LAWYERS AND LATTES

Dedicated to all my grandparents, who will always be missed.
Heinz, Carol, David, Gertrud and Derek.

CONTENTS

CHAPTER ONE

A new year, a new start, and one hell of a hangover. Lee's eyes blinked open and then quickly closed again as the light streamed in through the window and past her unclosed curtains. Her head felt a little like it was a spinning plate, about to be dropped; she took a deep breath and opened her eyes again. The year had certainly started off bright, with the morning sunlight casting beams of illumination across the floor that was littered with items of clothing. Lee blushed a little, remembering how they got there, not all that long after a midnight kiss at the bottom of the town.

She rolled over and grinned at the sight that greeted her, despite the nausea that made her feel a little like she were on a rolling ship. Lying in a shaft of sunlight, blond hair glittering, lay the handsome figure of James Knight. She placed a hand on his bare chest, knowing full well that he had contributed at least half of the trail of clothes on the floor and was therefore completely naked under the covers. This was the first time she had woken up with him next to her in her own flat, and she couldn't resist the urge to run a hand through his curly hair, with his head so close to hers on the pillow.

"Sorry," she murmured as his eyes flickered open. He

reached out an arm to pull her closer, and she found his face nuzzled into her neck. "I didn't mean to wake you."

"I'm off today," he said into her neck, the warmth of his breath making her shiver slightly as it tickled her delicate skin. "So I've got plenty of time to catch up on sleep. How are you feeling this morning?"

"Awful, if truth be told. I didn't think I drank that much... but I'm not as young as I used to be!"

James pulled away slightly so he could see her face, and moved his hand to stroke several strands of hair away from her eyes. "I didn't think you'd drunk that much, either," he said. "A bit tipsy, maybe, but not particularly drunk." His brow furrowed, and Lee stroked it with the tips of her fingers, confused as to why he was so concerned.

"Don't worry, I'm sure I'll live, hangovers only get worse once you're over thirty - you'll find out soon enough!" He didn't laugh, and Lee felt an unease in the pit of her stomach that she didn't think had anything to do with the amount - or lack thereof - of alcohol she had consumed the night before.

James ran a hand through his hair. "Last night..."

"I don't think I can think of words to describe last night," Lee said with a shy smile.

"I meant before we got back here."

"So did I, cheeky! Well, partially..."

James cleared his throat. "You do remember the whole night, don't you?"

"Of course I do, like I said, I wasn't that drunk."

James regarded her for a moment or two, not saying a word, just meeting her gaze. "You're definitely staying?"

Ahhh, Lee thought, so that was what was worrying him. It was so sweet she couldn't resist pressing her lips to his for a moment, and when she pulled away she grinned at him. "I'm staying. You can't get rid of me now - even if I'm so old that a couple of glasses of wine give me a terrible hangover."

James' grin lit up his eyes and rivalled Lee's at that comment, and he rolled so he hovered slightly above her. "You are young, and gorgeous, and I'm not planning on getting rid of you any time soon," he said, and now it was his turn to press his lips to hers, and her turn to feel as though she might dissolve into the air right there and then.

"Lee?" a voice shouted at the door, accompanied by a hammering that Lee's head could really have done without. "Lee, are you decent?"

Lee pulled away from James and glanced at him, and shook her head. "No!" she shouted back. There was what sounded like a laugh from the other side, then Gina's voice floated through the door once more. "I've made coffee, so make yourselves decent and come and get it while it's hot."

Lee grinned, even though James groaned as he rolled off her. Her flat mate Gina had struck her straight away as funny, direct and someone who took no rubbish - and that was exactly what she had turned out to be. Even though they'd only lived together for just over a month, they'd slipped into an easy rhythm that Lee couldn't remember feeling with anyone she'd lived with before - be it parents, siblings, house mates or partners.

They both scrambled around for some clothes to throw on; Lee had the luxury of her own pyjamas whereas James had to get properly dressed after being ill-equipped for the impromptu sleepover. The smell of coffee greeted them as they approached the kitchen, and it took Lee a minute or two to decide whether the smell made her more nauseous or improved things. She decided on it being an improvement and slid into the nearest chair, wrapping her hands around a mug.

"Well good morning love birds," Gina said with a self-satisfied smirk.

"Good morning Gina," James said with a grin; Lee just rolled her eyes. Gina and James talked for a few moments about the fireworks the previous night, the chilly start to the New Year and when he was next working, before Lee's brain kicked into gear; there were many people who needed to know about her snap decision, and one of the most important was sitting right in front of her. Waiting for a lull in the conversation, Lee felt James' hand on her knee and smiled.

"So, Gina," she said, deciding to address the issue head on. "I've made a decision."

"You're staying here forever and never leaving?" Gina asked, taking a bite of an apple and grinning at her own little joke.

"Well," Lee said, meeting James' eyes for a moment before turning back to Gina. "Yes, in a manner of speaking."

"You're staying?"

"If you don't mind! I know it was only going to be temporary, and you were going to run the cafe, but we talked last night and I realised-"

"Of course I don't mind! I've been waiting for you to realise you belonged here. I'm very glad you didn't disappear back to Bristol before realising it. Well done James - I'll chalk this one up to your influence!"

"Happy to take the credit," James said, taking a swig of the coffee Gina had placed in front of him. "Happy about a lot of things, actually..."

Gina made fake sick noises in the background; Lee rolled her eyes and told her to act her age, all with a big grin on her face.

After telling Gina of her plans to stay in Bristol, Lee knew there was only a limited amount of time left before she had to tell the other people in her life: her partners and her mother. She did consider messaging Nathan, but decided against it. After all, what difference did it make to him, really? And did he have a right to know what was going on in her life?

She was nervous about telling them for a myriad of reasons. She felt dizzy herself when she thought about the changes her life had gone through in the last six weeks - she wasn't sure how she could expect anyone else to keep up. And somewhere deep inside her, where she wouldn't quite even acknowledge its existence, there was the worry that someone (okay, she knew who it was likely to be - her mother) would suggest that this was all some sort of rebound. That she was making a huge mistake with her life; that she would ultimately regret it.

She knew in her heart that she didn't believe that to be true; that what she was feeling right now definitely didn't feel like some fling that was designed to move her past her disastrous failed marriage. But the possibility of hearing those words aloud... She put off the phone call for another day.

The bank holiday had allowed her to leave the cafe closed and succumb to her hangover, but the second of the month rolled round cold and bright, the first day of the year to open her lovely little cafe. Carol's Cafe (as she had named it, after her grandmother) had been her first solace when she'd arrived in Totnes at the beginning of December, fleeing a broken marriage and a cheating husband. When she'd found out the place was in desperate need of being taken over, she'd done so without much thought - and everything had very much snowballed from there.

James had worked the night of the first and so she had spent the evening alone, lamenting in the ridiculous fact that she missed him at the same time as enjoying a girly evening with Gina and the full width of the bed to herself. The very early morning alarm hadn't been quite so welcome, but a hot shower and a large mug of coffee later and she felt ready to tackle the world. Gina was still asleep when she left - they'd decided a rota would be made later on in the week since they would both be running the cafe now - and Lee slipped out in her thick coat and paint-splat scarf, deciding to walk down the steep hill instead of being lazy and getting the car out. Besides, she very much hoped James might stop by at some point and offer her a lift...

It wasn't until she was halfway down the hill that she remembered with a disappointing jolt that James was meant to be working late that night... perhaps she wouldn't get to see him at all that day - not a happy thought.

Once the doors were unlocked, the familiar routine of setting up the cafe seemed to whiz by, and before long the doors were open onto a particularly sleepy looking high street. Lee couldn't blame the residents; if she hadn't been working she would definitely have still been asleep at this hour.

Her first customer of the day surprised her somewhat, for she hadn't been seen out and about this early in the morning since giving up that same cafe. Val, the previous lease owner and surprisingly sprightly elderly resident of Totnes, had a big grin on her face when she saw Lee.

"You didn't disappear at midnight then?" she asked.

"I decided you were right, Val," Lee said, beginning to make her a coffee without being asked. "You can make your own reality - and this was what I chose. So, I'm afraid, there's no getting rid of me for a while at least!"

"And does young PC Knight have anything to do with this sudden change of heart?"

Lee blushed, and turned to froth the milk. When she

turned back, Val's piercing eyes were still on her, and she couldn't avoid answering. "Maybe," she admitted.

"Life in a small town Lee - nothing stays secret for long, I'm afraid, although I don't know why you'd want to keep it a secret!"

Lee shrugged, unsure if she could put her feelings into words, unsure whether she even wanted to share the emotion that was bubbling up inside her. "I don't want to jinx things," she finally confessed, and was a little taken aback when Val reached over and patted her on the hand.

"That's a load of nonsense, dear, if you don't mind me saying. You follow your heart and it won't matter if the whole town knows - besides, James has lived here long enough that he'll know full well that you can't keep anything from the town!"

Other customers appeared before Lee really had a chance to respond, but she smiled a little at Val's words and got on with making teas, coffees and hot chocolates, her worries about 'jinxing' the relationship certainly soothed a little.

The busyness of the cafe made the time disappear, and before she knew it Gina had arrived and they were slap bang in the middle of the lunch time rush, serving takeaway teas and coffees to workers in nearby shops and offices, and plenty of cakes too. They had discussed serving hot food, as Val used to do when she owned it, but had decided it was probably better to walk before they could run. Besides, neither of them were particularly great cooks, and hiring anyone else wasn't on the cards at the moment.

LAWYERS AND LATTES

Lee was busy cleaning the milk steamer while waiting for the coffee to grind when she heard the bell above the door jingle for what seemed like the millionth time that day. She didn't even turn her head to welcome the customer, trusting that Gina would do so; it wasn't until Gina cleared her throat in what seemed like an overly dramatic way that Lee turned to see who had entered.

She found herself grinning without even thinking about it, and saw that he was the same, and that burnt away a lot of the strange anxiousness she had been feeling for the last day or so.

"Hey," she said.

"Hey." Lee was vaguely aware of Gina busying herself making the next batch of coffees with the freshly ground beans, and she felt suddenly like an awkward teenager with her first boyfriend, unsure of quite what the right thing to say or do was. They both took a step towards the counter at the same time, so that it was the only thing between them. James leant over, clearly intent on kissing her, and Lee didn't need to think before she leant towards him too. Had she been thinking about the cafe full of customers around them, she might have considered their kiss a little too deep and a little too long to be so thoroughly observed - but her mind was not on such matters at that moment in time. No, it was on his lips as they pressed against hers, his hand as it touched against her cheek, the feel of his sharply creased uniform beneath her palm...

And then one - or both of them - remembered where they were, and they pulled apart with a blush from Lee

9

and a hasty cough to hide his grin on James' part.

Lee felt as though the cafe had gone silent around her, and when she dared to peek past James' fine, uniformed form she found that she was right - everyone in the small cafe seemed to be looking at them or pretending they hadn't just been looking at them

For a second, Lee closed her eyes and then snapped them back to meet James'; seeing that a grin still played on his lips, she tried to let her embarrassment at being the centre of attention fade away and allow the tingling memory of that kiss to be the only thing on her mind.

Slowly the buzz returned to the cafe, and although Lee was fairly sure that buzz was now about her and James, she decided not to listen in.

"Sorry," James said, running a hand through his hair as he always seemed to when he was a bit unsure of himself.

"For making us the talk of the town?" Lee asked, but there was a twinkle in her eye as she said it.

"Couldn't help myself," he said.

"Well, I guess there'll be no keeping our relationship under wraps in this place anyway," she said, echoing the earlier wisdom Val had shared with her.

"Did you want to?" His eyebrows knotted together slightly, and Lee once again got the feeling that this man in front of her wasn't quite as confident as she might have imagined.

"I guess I'm just not used to everyone taking an interest in my romantic life," she said. "Other than when everyone I knew found out my husband had cheated on me, I guess. Sorry, sorry, dark joke." She felt amazed that she could make a joke - dark or otherwise - about something that, not long ago would have had her hysterically crying. She smiled to lighten the mood. "And you never have to apologise for kissing me."

"Good," James said, taking the coffee that Gina wordlessly handed to him. "Have you rung your partners yet?"

Lee took a deep breath. "No. I was going to tackle that tonight, since you're working late." Once the words were out, she realised that was based on an assumption that they would be spending the night together every night - something that they had never discussed. Just because she was moving here did not mean, she told herself, that she should treat this like a ready-made long-term relationship. That seemed like a recipe for disaster.

"I'm sure they'll understand," he said, glancing at the clock before sipping his coffee.

Lee laughed. "I'm not so sure they will. They thought I was having a breakdown when I came down here in the first place. But, it has to be done."

"I've got to head off in a minute," James said. "I'm sorry - I wanted to see you, but I've only got ten minutes before I need to be back at the station."

"Thanks for coming," Lee said, twirling a sugar packet in between her fingers.

"Thanks for the kiss, and the coffee."

"Happy to help." She giggled, and when James bent to kiss her on the cheek she felt a shiver go through her.

"See you tomorrow?" he asked, putting his hat on as he stood up.

"I'll be here!"

"I finish at four. I'll pick you up?"

"Always good to save my legs the walk home."

"And take you out - stop teasing me!" James said, replacing a wayward strand of her hair behind one ear before ducking out of the door. Lee watched him leave, watched him turn and wave through the window, watched him cross the road and walk towards his parked police car.

"You've got it bad," a voice behind her said, and it broke her reverie. She turned to find Gina, with her purple-tinted hair scraped up in a ponytail and her lip piercing bobbing as she laughed.

"Oh, shut up," Lee said, the smile not leaving her face.

"Honestly, if you didn't deserve to be so happy I'd think it was all rather sickening. I'll need to have words with young PC Knight... if he hurts you, he'll have me to answer to."

And even though opening up her heart so soon after having it smashed to pieces was the thing Lee had been most afraid of, she was fairly sure that James would not hurt her. And if he did, she almost felt sorry for him, having to face an angry Gina.

CHAPTER TWO

Gina had plans that evening with Lydia, and Lee settled in for a quiet night. She'd spent little time alone since she'd appeared in a whirlwind of misery at the beginning of December, and she found she wasn't used to it. She fidgeted on the sofa and changed the channel twenty-five times before acknowledging that the real reason she was so antsy was that she was putting off making that phone call. The one to her work partners that she knew wouldn't go down well.

Wrapped up in a blanket and with a glass of wine in front of her, Lee stared at her phone screen for a full five minutes before hitting dial. It was six-thirty in the evening, and yet she was still trying the office number: one, it would be much easier if they were both together; two, she expected them to be at work still. After all, she'd rarely left the office before seven.

"Hello?" The voice picking up the phone did not reel off the usual greeting - perhaps because it was outside office hours - but Lee recognised it immediately as Tania.

With a deep breath and the knowledge that there was no turning back, Lee spoke. "Hi, Tania, it's Lee."

"Lee! We were expecting you in today, did we get our

wires crossed?"

Oh boy. No, Lee thought... the wires had just drastically changed.

"Where are you living now? We could pop over tonight if you like, catch you up on everything. It feels like forever since we saw you last!"

Lee let her babble on for a few minutes, planning her next words in her head until she got the opportunity to speak again. "Tania, is Gemma around still? I'd like to talk to you both."

Tania's tone changed slightly, and Lee could imagine the confused look on her face. "She's just heading out, I'll see if I can catch her." Silence, and then the clear sound of being on speaker phone.

"Hi, Lee," Gemma's voice floated through the phone. "Happy new year!"

"Happy new year," Lee answered. "I'm sorry to do this over the phone, but I'm not actually in Bristol to do it in person." She pushed through, needing to get the words out before their protests began. "I've decided I need to stay down here - for me. I can't move back to Bristol, not for the foreseeable future anyway. And so... I need to leave the firm."

There was silence for a moment on the other end of the line, and Lee gave them a second or two to process what she had just said.

"You're leaving law?" Tania asked, sounding incredulous.

"I don't know. For now... yes. Maybe not forever - but I need to start again, and that means not moving back to Bristol, and not coming back to practise law. I'm so sorry..."

"We don't want you to be sorry, Lee," Gemma said. "But is this really what you want? A break, I get it, your life has been turned upside down, everyone would need some time to get over that. But leaving your home city, leaving the law firm you're partner in, making it permanent? You can't just put your life on hold."

Lee had known there would be opposition to what she was saying - hell, if she'd heard someone else deciding to give up the career they'd worked so many years for, she probably would have given them a harder time than Gemma was doing now.

"I know how mental this all sounds, believe me - but I'm not putting my life on hold, I promise. I've just decided to start my life again, here." She hadn't really thought too deeply about her career in law - but there was no reason she had to give up on it all together, just because she was leaving Phillips, Jones and Sharp, just because she was leaving Bristol in her past.

She heard a sigh that she thought was Tania. "So... you want leave the partnership? Permanently?"

Lee felt her breath catch in her throat: permanently. She guessed that was what she was saying - but permanent was a hell of commitment. What if things didn't work out with James? What if Gina got sick of living with her? What if the cafe didn't turn a profit? There were so many unknowns, so little certainty about this path she'd chosen to follow...

"I don't know whether things will work out, permanently," she admitted - but then she'd thought things in Bristol would be permanent, and look how that had turned out. "But I know it's not fair to you to keep you hanging on, waiting for me to come back. I'm going to give 'permanent' a good go down here - and so I need to leave the partnership."

"Okay. If that's what you want, Lee, we'll get it sorted. We'll miss you, though."

Lee swallowed. "I'll miss you too, both of you. I've loved working with you both..." She could feel the tears welling up in her eyes and cut her sentence short to try to make it to the end of the conversation without sobbing.

"We'll be in touch, then, Lee," Tania said, and although Lee knew the conversation felt stilted and awkward, she couldn't find a way to make it less so.

"Speak soon..." she said, and before the line clicked off she thought she heard Gemma speaking to Tania. She quickly hung up - she didn't think she wanted to know what they were saying about her. Pulling the blanket more tightly around her and taking a large sip of her glass of wine, Lee decided she didn't have the emotional strength right now to phone her mother and let her know of the changes to her plans. She knew already what her mother would say; the range of ways she would try to talk her out of it, the many seeds of doubt she would sow in her mind. An email, she decided, would suffice - and not just because she knew her mother checked her emails once a week at best...

For simplicity's sake - and to get a chance at having someone on her side - she decided at the last minute to add her sister in to the email too. Typing on her phone reminded her sharply that at some point in the not-too-distant future, she really needed to go back to Bristol and collect her things - her clothes, her laptop, her passport - all the things she had left that night when she'd abandoned the city that was once her home.

Hiya,

Hope you are both having a great start to the New Year. It was really snowy here but we haven't had any for a few days - it's just very cold! The cafe's busy so far even with it being January.

I made a decision a few days ago that I wanted to let you both know about. I've decided that I'm going to stay here, in Totnes, and not move back to Bristol. I know it was only going to be temporary, but for now I feel like this is where I belong. I hope you'll understand and support me in this - and I'd love to see you both soon.

Lots of love,
Lee xx

She hit send without even reading it back, in case she changed her mind, and then took a deep, calming breath. They knew. They all knew. Anyone who needed to know was now aware that Shirley Davis lived in Totnes, and was not returning to Bristol any time soon.

She felt a sick feeling in the pit of her stomach as she contemplated this massive change, and was in desperate need of one or two more deep breaths.

CHAPTER THREE

Two weeks into January and Lee had received a positive email from her sister regarding her move, with a promise to visit soon - but nothing yet from her mother. She was trying to put it to the back of her mind, but it loomed there often whenever she let her mind wander. It was a horrible feeling, waiting for someone to disapprove of you.

Most of the time, however, her mind wasn't able to wander. The cafe kept her days busy, and James kept most evenings busy, with more dates than she had been on in years. They'd been out to dinner three nights, each time somewhere small and new with local produce and a romantic ambiance. Lee felt she needed to pinch herself on these nights; she felt like she were someone else entirely, living a fairy tale that she had never imagined for herself. One night they went to a tiny cinema with two screens, and laughed over their popcorn at an awkward teenage couple who seemed to be on their first date.

"You make me feel like a teenager," Lee said that night as they strolled gloved-hand in gloved-hand through the chilly night air and back to the car. "I feel like all of this is new, and exciting, and I don't quite know what to expect."

"Isn't that what makes it fun?" James asked with a

grin, ducking into a nearby shop doorway and kissing her away from the rain and the passing strangers.

And he was right. Lee couldn't remember the last time she'd grinned so much at someone texting her, or made mistakes at ridiculously simple tasks because she'd been daydreaming. Apart from that cloud of her mother's comments - or lack thereof - life seemed pretty perfect.

They wandered past the dark windows of the cafe, and Lee felt that same burst of pride in her chest when she saw the sign above it: *Carol's Cafe*. She'd done this, she was making a success of this - and she thought she was almost more proud of this than when she'd qualified as a lawyer.

"Did you hear back from your mum yet?" James asked as they reached the car. Lee felt her breath suck in even as he opened the passenger door for her.

"No," she said. "Not yet. I'm half expecting her to turn up at any moment and try to shake some sense into me…"

"Well, you have already met my parents, after all!" James said with a grin, giving her hand a squeeze before starting the engine.

"I'm not sure you want to meet my mum when she's on a mission to tell me I'm making a mistake with my life…"

"Do you think you're making a mistake with your life?" James asked, not taking his eyes off the road, but Lee let herself glance over at him and thought she saw a little tension around his eyes.

"I really don't," she said with a grin. "Now, are we going back to my place or yours?"

James laughed, and indicated right, driving away from town in the direction of his picturesque cottage.

They stepped through the door onto the polished wooden floors, and Lee glanced around, marvelling at how tidy he seemed to keep it. She supposed he was currently spending most of his hours at work or with her - but still, it was definitely neater than her and Gina's place, although she had to admit Gina was the messier of the two. The Christmas decorations were gone, and Lee slipped off her heels so as not to mark the floors before following James into the kitchen.

"Wine?" he asked, taking a bottle of white from the fridge.

"I'll leave it thanks - is it boring if I have a cup of tea?"

"Showing your age!" James said with a laugh, but replaced the bottle without opening it.

"Oh ha, ha, very funny. Doesn't mean you can't have some, though - I just feel a bit off, don't fancy it. Too many early mornings, I reckon."

"Or too many late nights..."

"And whose fault is that?!"

They both laughed, a care free sound that filled the kitchen right up to the exposed wooden beams.

They chatted over tea (James declined to have a glass of wine on his own) and sighed at how early their respective alarms needed to be set the next morning: James' for a funeral of a family member that he'd never met but had promised to take his mum and dad to, and Lee's for her usual opening shift in cafe.

"I could do with a lie-in," Lee said. "I'm exhausted."

"Can Gina not open up?"

"I don't want to change the plan this late - but maybe the next morning, give me a chance to catch up on sleep."

Lee's phone buzzed in her pocket, and James took the opportunity to wash up the cups while she checked it. She grinned as she watched him for a moment - she guessed that attention to detail was why his house was always tidy. At her and Gina's flat she knew those mugs would have sat there for a couple of hours at least.

Then she looked down at the screen at felt the smile freeze on her face. *New message from Nathan.*

She hadn't heard from him for a while, but the sight of his name on her phone still made her heart start to hammer and her blood chill. She glanced up: James hadn't noticed her freezing. Without really wanting to, she clicked on *read.* She couldn't help it; she couldn't leave it there to fester.

Have filed divorce papers. Need an address for you. N.

She took a deep, shuddering breath and, without thinking, responded.

You have the address already. I've not moved.

No more words were needed. She didn't even add an initial on the end - he knew who it was who was messaging. Of course he did. Who else would he be messaging about divorce papers? He might well have slept with whoever he liked, but he was only married to one of them, that she was sure of.

Well, not for much longer.

"Everything okay?" She'd been staring angrily into space for some time, she realised, and James had finished his tidying up and had obviously noticed her carefree mood had evaporated as quickly as the unexpected snow had melted.

"Just..." She didn't really know what to say; she didn't want to ruin what was blossoming between her and James with this from her past - and yet there was no way she couldn't feel strange at the message telling her that her marriage was soon to be legally over. Even though it had been over in her heart the second she'd walked in on Nathan with *her*... "Nothing important."

"Really? You don't look like it's nothing important." Her eyes met his, and she felt so much warmth coming from them that she thought that maybe she could share just a little of her strange pain without jeopardising their romance.

"It's weird to mention," she said apologetically. "But it was a message telling me divorce papers have been filed." She avoided saying his name; it felt less personal that way. Nevertheless, she felt tears pool in the corners of her eyes and blinked furiously to dispel them. She'd cried enough over that bastard, that was for sure, and she didn't know why the tears had to make an appearance again now. "At least I know lots of lawyers," she said, trying to joke past the moment.

James leant over the table and took a strand of Lee's blonde hair between his fingers, gently placing it behind her ear.

"Lee," he said softly. "It's okay to feel sad. It's okay to be upset when you're told divorce papers are being filed. It's okay to feel miserable about it."

"It's not okay to be like this in front of you, though," Lee said, rubbing the tears from her eyes when blinking didn't quite do the job. "I should go - I feel really weird about this, and it's not your problem to deal with."

"Lee." He was in front of her now, kneeling on the floor so he didn't tower above her seated form. Lee placed a hand in his hair, feeling the soft curls between her fingers, and tried to smile. "If you want to go, I'll drive you home now. But don't feel you have to go on my account. I wish you weren't sad, I wish you hadn't been hurt like this - but you don't need to hide it from me. You can be sad here, with me."

Their eyes met once more and Lee found she could smile, even if tears were still partially obscuring her eyes. "How on earth did I meet someone so good?" she whispered, and she leant forward to press her lips gently to his, feeling a tear drop onto their lips as she did. She sighed, feeling frustrated at the lack of control she seemed to have over her emotions.

"I've got my flaws, believe me," James said when their lips broke apart. "And I'd rather be with you even if you're sad than without you." He ran a hand through his hair. "Sorry, that was cheesy - and maybe a bit too much. I find it hard to make myself slow down when I'm with you, to remember that you've just come out of a long relationship, a marriage…"

"I haven't seen any flaws," Lee answered. "And I promise I'll tell you, if I need to slow down."

They kissed there in the kitchen, hands in each other's hair, lips and tongues burning a pathway that seemed to make the sadness melt into the background.

It was much later, when they were wrapped in each other's arms in bed, on the edge of sleep, when Lee heard him whisper words that she suspected he wouldn't have said under the bright kitchen lights.

"Don't walk away and leave me without any warning…"

It was a second before the words registered in her sleepy mind; this plea to not just disappear, a plea she couldn't really understand. But she could roll into his arms even tighter, she could wrap her arms around him, and she could murmur back: "I never would. I promise."

CHAPTER FOUR

It was the first day of February, and Lee found she had to drag herself out of bed in rather a foul mood. She couldn't put her finger on why - the early mornings were normal for her, and she didn't usually resent them - but for the last few days it had just seemed liked such hard work. It didn't help that James had been working nights for the whole week, she supposed, and she had barely seen him, let alone curled up in his arms at night (something which had become a fairly regular occurrence.) They had a date planned for two days' time, but she still found herself feeling unreasonably irritated by it all. She sat on the edge of the bed, her head in her hands for a moment, willing herself to get going and go and shower. That would make everything better, she was sure; wash away this fog in her mind and nausea in her stomach.

When she eventually made it into the living room, after giving herself a stern talking-to, she was surprised to find Gina already up and doing some sort of yoga poses in the middle of the floor.

"Morning," she said, heading straight for the kettle.

"You're opening up today, aren't you?" Gina asked, as the tips of her toes seemed to touch the back of her head in a position Lee was sure she had never been able to manage - not even as a child.

"Mmmhmmm."

"Good - I was worried it was me, when I saw you weren't up yet."

"Having trouble getting going," Lee said. "Which clearly isn't the case for you!"

"It was going to be a New Year's resolution," Gina said, bending into yet another impossible-looking pose. "But I'm a bit late starting!"

By the time Lee had reached the cafe, following a very speedy shower and a brisk walk down the hill, her mood had lightened a little, although the fogginess and queasiness didn't seem to wash away as easily. Still, she felt the familiar feeling of peace as she unlocked the doors, put the chairs down and began the daily routines that she already felt she could do in her sleep. The coffee was on, the cakes set out on their trays, the tablecloths straightened and the door sign switched to 'open'.

By ten, the cafe was full of a cheerful buzz that made Lee smile, despite herself. There was a young family in the corner that seemed to have become semi-regulars - mum, dad and two under-fives. Then an older gentleman with a walker who always took the first table by the door, and a couple of unknowns in fairly smart clothing. Val appeared in the doorway not long after, and Lee grinned and began to make her usual coffee.

"Nice and busy, just what I like to see," Val said, glancing around before taking a seat at the table nearest the counter.

"Oh, we're doing okay," Lee said, wiping a few errant droplets of milk off the side before walking round the counter to put the coffee on the table. She was about to sit down and join Val for a moment or two, when the bell on the door chimed again and another customer stepped in.

"No rest for the wicked," she said with a grin, and stepped back behind the counter.

"What can I get you?" she asked the tall red-head who was standing before her. A large messenger bag was slung over one of her shoulders, trapping a few of the dark red curls beneath the strap. The woman glanced at the menu on the blackboard behind Lee before answering.

"Didn't this place used to do food?"

Lee didn't feel her tone was particularly cordial, but she plastered a smile onto her face before responding. "Yes, but it's under new ownership and it's strictly coffees, teas, cakes and pastries right now."

"Oh."

"What are *you* doing in here?" They both turned to the source of the voice: the normally smiling, normally sweet-as-sugar Val. Lee's eyes widened in shock; the woman in question narrowed hers a little.

"Just visiting the area," she said, running a hand through those long, curly locks. "Seeing how it's doing."

"The *area* is just fine, no thanks to you. And it certainly doesn't need any interference." Lee couldn't help but feel that she was missing so many parts to this conversation. While it was obvious they weren't actually talking about the area, she had no clue what the actual topic of conversation was. And it wasn't good for business, Val being so rude...

"Can I get you a coffee?" she asked, a false cheeriness to her voice. The woman didn't turn her head back to face Lee; instead she kept her eyes on Val's.

"I think perhaps I'll go elsewhere."

"Don't meddle, Lottie. You did enough damage last time."

The buzz in the cafe seemed to have evaporated, and Lee couldn't help but think that everyone had stopped to listen to this exchange. Hell, who was she kidding, it was a small town - of course they were listening.

The door closed behind Lottie and her messenger bag, and Lee stood, slightly open mouthed, unsure as to what she had just witnessed.

"Val!" she finally said, when a little of the noise had returned to the cafe, and they weren't being watched quite so closely. "What on earth was that all about?"

"Just someone from the past," she said, looking irritated still. "It's not up to me to share it with you anyway."

Lee was thrown by that one for a minute; Val had certainly never snapped at her before, and what on earth did she mean about sharing it?

She pottered around behind the counter for a few minutes, letting the words sink in and Val calm down. When she looked back at the table, Val was watching her.

"I didn't mean to be short with you, dear. I'm sorry. An

old woman can get worked up about these things."

"But what things?" Lee asked, perplexed. "And how on earth could they involve me?"

"It's not my place to fill you in, dear," she repeated, but a little more kindly this time.

Lee's head was whirring away, trying to solve the puzzle. How could that woman's identity be linked to her in anyway? She barely knew anyone down here, properly anyway. There was Val, there was Gina, there was James...

Oh. God.

"Is that – was that her?" she asked, aware her words made little sense, but struggling to find the right ones. "Is that the woman James was going to marry? The one that left a week before the wedding?"

Slowly, reluctantly, Val nodded – and Lee felt the sickness in the pit of her stomach take an even tighter hold.

Gina seemed to float through the door at twelve; clearly her new yoga regime was having a positive effect on her. Lee, on the other hand, felt anything other than floaty. She felt as though she was serving in a daze, with a heavy weight resting in the pit of her stomach and a million thoughts running through her brain. She wished she hadn't been thrown so much by her morning visitor and Val's revelation. Seeing the ex of a guy she'd been dating all of six weeks shouldn't make her feel like she needed a lie down away from the rest of the room - should it?

"What's up?" Gina said, the second she'd looked at Lee.

"Nothing," Lee lied, wiping down the milk frother and not quite meeting Gina's eyes. "Just feeling a bit under the weather."

"Still? Lee, that's been a couple of weeks now, why don't you get an appointment with a doctor?"

"It's nothing major, honest." She didn't feel she could share the fact that James' jilter seemed to be back in town and, if Lee had read between the lines well enough, asking about him. Partly because it wasn't her information to share, and partly because she couldn't seem to wrap her head round it - and how she felt about it.

"Go home, have a lie down then, at least," Gina said, rolling up the sleeves of her denim jacket and gently pushing Lee out of the way.

"I don't want to leave you if it's busy..." Lee said, but without any real conviction.

"Don't be ridiculous, we've both managed on our own perfectly well before. Scram, get yourself to bed. Have you got the car?"

Lee shook her head, regretting her decision to enjoy the fresh air that morning. "I'll be okay," she said; Gina didn't look entirely convinced, but ushered Lee out with her coat and bag, reassuring her once more that everything would be fine with the cafe.

The hill seemed more like a mountain at that moment as Lee contemplated it from the bottom. She began to trudge up it in a daze, questioning why on earth she was feeling so messed up. She was the one who had said that they couldn't be serious, she was the one that said about taking it slow, and they hadn't even been together for two months. And yet... and yet seeing a woman who had hurt him so badly, a woman that he possibly still had feelings for, in her little cafe... well, it was making everything hurt in a way that she hadn't expected to happen so soon after the end of her marriage.

Around halfway up the hill, the thoughts began to make her head spin faster than she could keep up with. She leant in a doorway, head dropping, and tried to take some deep breaths. Was this a panic attack? Her eyes closed and she pictured James, a man she was worried she'd lost her heart to before it was ready to be lost again, and the woman he had hoped to marry. She pictured the man she *had* married, the man who had turned her life upside down in such a violent way that she felt she'd lost all identity, that she'd had to start from scratch. It was something she didn't think she could survive twice.

She pictured that blonde, the one who had shattered her illusions about her own life - and was promptly sick all over the street outside the sweet shop.

It was a testament to how friendly the residents of Totnes seemed to be that no-one screamed at her for such a display on a high street in front of a place of business. She knew, as she sat in the back room of the sweet shop on a rickety three-legged stool, that she would have been none too pleased if someone had vomited right outside her cafe's front door. But here she sat, head still swimming a little, clasping a glass of cold water that she had kindly been given and trying desperately to apologise.

"It was an accident, dear," the elderly gentleman who seemed to run the shop replied. "My wife's thrown a bucket of water over it, one good rainfall and it'll be completely forgotten. Now, aren't you the young maid who took over the cafe at the bottom of the hill?"

The word 'maid' threw her for a second, before she remembered hearing another local use it when talking about a young woman - and his thick Devon accent made it sound less of an unusual choice of word.

"That's me," she said weakly, sipping on the water and wishing she could be at home, in bed. "And I am really sorry, I don't know what came over me, I've been feeling under the weather for a couple of weeks and then I got some news and-" She was babbling, she knew it, and she clamped her lips shut before she could reel off her life story to a couple of strangers who had probably witnessed her throwing up.

"Been feeling rotten for a couple of weeks? Oh that won't do," said the man's wife, suddenly by his side. "You need to get yourself down to the doctors, get checked over."

"I'm fine, honestly-"

"You most definitely are not fine! Give them a ring now and get an appointment, or I'll do it for you. The receptionist is our grand-daughter so I'd have no trouble getting you one."

Feeling beaten, Lee picked up her phone and dialled the number that the woman recited. She didn't have the energy to argue and, besides, maybe there was something wrong with her. Something more than being an emotional wreck...

"Hello, I'm wondering if you had any doctors' appointments for today? Yes, I know it's late..." She was glad now that her mother had always drilled in to her that the first thing to be done when moving in somewhere new was to register with the doctor - but even so, she didn't rate her chances of getting a same day appointment after lunch time.

"Pass me that phone," the grey-haired lady said, taking Lee's phone without much of a pause. "Shelley? It's your grandmother Jonie here. Yes, yes, never mind all that. This young lady needs an appointment today, no messing around. Ten minutes? Great she'll be there."

And with that the phone was passed back to Lee, who gave over her details a little in awe of Jonie, who must've been seventy if she were a day.

"Thank you, I don't know how-"

"There was a cancellation," Jonie said, seeming to know what Lee was about to say before she'd even said it. "Now, you'd better get going, it's only a five minute walk. Do you think you'll be okay?"

"Yes, yes, thank you," she said, and as she was ushered out of the door she felt an overwhelming sense of being completely out of control of everything in her life. It was a feeling she had felt before, that was true - but not for a few weeks. Following the directions that Jonie's husband had given her, she wandered in the direction of the doctors' surgery - trying her very hardest not to think about how her life could possibly shift seismically all over again if James were to reunite with Lottie.

On the front desk was a woman Lee thought to be younger than herself, with ringlety blonde hair and a bright pink headband.

"Mrs Jones, isn't it?" the woman on the desk said, and Lee nodded, wishing she hadn't registered in her married name. "I'm Shelley - it seems you know my grandparents!"

Lee nodded again, but didn't speak; as lovely as it could be that everyone knew each other, she felt that in this moment of time, sat in a doctors' waiting room, she just wanted a little peace, quiet, and anonymity.

Her lack of conversation didn't seem to deter Shelley. "Anyway, doctor's running about five minutes late, so you shouldn't be waiting too long. Take a seat, enjoy a magazine, and we'll call you when it's your appointment."

"Thanks," Lee said, and took a seat next to the bathroom door, just in case the sickness hit again. She didn't expect it to, however; she was fairly confident that her problem was emotional, not physical, and she was exerting great effort to *not think* about things that might set her off.

"So, Mrs Jones, how can I help you?" the doctor asked. She smiled, and Lee opened her mouth to speak - and then wasn't sure where to start.

"It's a long story," she said - and it all came flooding out. The insane hours she'd been working, Nathan cheating on her, the move, the cafe, James, the uncertainty of it all. Then the heavy, sick feeling, the exhaustion, the vomiting that morning. She barely breathed as it all spilled out, and when she finally took a breath and realised she was crying, she was shocked to find it had only taken her five minutes to share the most mortifying details of her life.

"I'm sorry," she said, taking a proffered tissue and wiping at her eyes.

"No need to be. It sounds like you've been through the emotional wringer lately, Mrs - Shirley." Lee cringed a little - Shirley made her shudder almost as much as Mrs Jones did.

"I do think these symptoms could all be stress related, but I want to rule out a couple of other things first, if that's okay?"

Lee nodded, not really trusting herself to speak in case she had another attack of verbal diarrhoea.

"So, are you on any medication at all?"

"No."

"And when was your last period?"

Lee paused to think; it had never been something that was particularly predictable; it appeared when it decided to, lasted for five days of misery then disappeared again. She'd definitely had one since she'd been in Totnes, though...she remembered borrowing from Gina's sanitary stash.

"About half way through December, I think."

The doctor tapped away on the keyboard for a second.

"Shirley, have you considered you could be pregnant?"

Pregnant? The word had never been close to her mind, not since her world had fallen apart and the idea of children had become a distant dream once again. "Pregnant?"

"It's been 7 weeks since your last period…"

"They're always erratic," Lee responded, trying to let the word settle in her mind.

"Even so, it would explain some of these symptoms. Let's do a test, shall we, no point thinking about possibilities when we could know in a few minutes."

If Lee had been feeling out of control before, it was nothing to how she felt now.

Sickness overwhelmed her once more - but luckily this time it was in the bathroom as she gave her sample, and so she didn't make such a fool of herself. Not thinking was proving more and more difficult by the minute.

The two women sat in silence as they waited for the strip to reveal all. Lee focussed on her breathing and on not contemplating any what-ifs, for the minutes that it took. She thought she must have been making the whole surgery run late, but she couldn't quite find it in herself to worry.

As the waiting became unbearable, she closed her eyes and revelled in the darkness.

"Shirley?"

"It's Lee," she responded, opening her eyes to find the doctor's brown eyes looking right into hers.

"Sorry, Lee. Are you feeling okay?"

"Just tell me..."

"You are pregnant, Lee. And if your period date was around the 15th of December, it would put you at about seven weeks."

The world swam in front of Lee's eyes, and she promptly vomited into a conveniently placed bin.

CHAPTER FIVE

Lee didn't think she could have told someone how she got home from the doctors' that day if they'd asked. All she knew was that she found herself outside the front door, key hovering in the lock, wondering how on earth this possibility had never occurred to her.

It took a few moments for her to actually manage to unlock the door and step inside. Dumping her keys and her handbag on the dining table, she headed for the sofa and wrapped herself up in a blanket, closing her eyes and letting the overwhelming mix of thoughts and feelings wash over her like a tidal wave.

Pregnant.

Six months ago she would have been secretly overjoyed by the news, even though they'd not been trying. It was, after all, something she'd wanted for a very long time.

But six months ago her life had a path, a plan. She'd followed everything in the right order: meet a guy, get a career, get married, buy a house - having a baby would have just been the logical next step in the journey. Now her life was a mixed up jumble and, as much as she was enjoying it, she certainly didn't have a clear cut future lined up. This was certainly not planned; yes, she'd stopped taking the pill when she and Nathan had split, but it wasn't like she and James hadn't been careful...

But not careful enough.

Thinking of James was enough to give her a headache. The fragility of their situation had hit her that morning, when she'd realised what a spin the appearance of his ex had sent her in to. And of course, it made sense; he had history with this woman, a past, a planned future, a planned wedding for goodness sake. They were things she didn't have with him. She had a great time, they had amazing sex, there was chemistry, for sure - but no real history. Not like he must have with her...

And now fragility was even more of a concern.

Pregnant.

Even now she couldn't quite believe it, even with the doctor and test telling her exactly that. She couldn't be happy, because it was all out of order. Could she do this on her own, if it came to it?

So much to think about.

As if to force her brain to pause at that moment, there was a sudden knock on the door. She debated ignoring it for a second, but thought better of it.

The sight of him made her want to cry.

"Hey," he said, concern colouring his face. "Gina rang me, said you were ill and not answering her messages." He walked in before she could invite him to, and she closed the door behind him, not quite knowing what to say.

"I didn't realise she'd messaged," she answered truthfully.

"Come, sit back down, you look really pale." He took her by the hand and led her over to the sofa. "Sorry you're feeling rubbish."

Lee curled up into the arm he held out, feeling safe and warm in his embrace even as she knew it might only be temporary. "You didn't have to rush round."

"Gina was worried you hadn't made it home. I was worried…" He pressed his lips to the top of her head, then rooted around in his pocket. "I'd better text her - I promised I would and, well, I wouldn't like to get on the wrong side of her."

He fired off a quick message - *I'm here, she's okay, thanks for ringing* - before putting it back in his pocket. "You should've told me you felt ill, I could have picked you up."

"I knew you were working," she said, aware of the stiffness of his police uniform beneath her hand. "I didn't want to be a bother… I just feel really rotten." She paused. "Maybe I ate something bad." It was a lie, and she knew it, but she couldn't tell him the truth just yet. She needed to get her own head round it all first… and see where they stood.

"James," she said, swallowing a little. "I need to tell you something."

He looked at her expectantly.

With a deep breath, she spat out the words as though they were the thing making her ill - which she now knew was not the case. "Lottie came in the cafe today. She's back in Totnes... for now."

She saw the colour drain from his face; she felt him freeze next to her. And that she could understand; she was sure that, even in the future, the mention of Nathan's name would be enough to make her blood run cold.

"James?" she prompted after a few moments of silence.

His tongue dampened his bottom lip. "Sorry. Just... wasn't expecting that. How... how did you know it was her?"

"Val," she said with a weak smile. "Small town charm, eh - everyone knows everyone's business."

He laughed, but there was no real mirth in it.

Lee closed her eyes and took a deep breath - partly to settle her nerves and partly to settle her stomach.

"I know this will have thrown you for six. I get it. You don't need to hide your emotions from me."

An echo of words he'd said to her previously - and yet she knew it would hurt her to hear him speak of a former love. Did it hurt him, when she mentioned Nathan?

"Thank you..." he said slowly. "I think... I think I just need to process. Is that okay?"

Lee nodded. It had to be.

"Do you need anything right now?" he asked, and her heart melted at his sweetness even in his own moment of turmoil.

"Just sleep," she said, releasing him for now. "You go.

Honestly. We'll talk tomorrow, yeah?"

He pressed a long, hard kiss to her forehead - and then he was gone.

Lee curled up in a ball under the blanket and cried tears that wouldn't solve anything at all.

CHAPTER SIX

Lee must've fallen asleep, for when she opened her eyes it was dark outside and Gina was quietly cooking in the kitchen. Her eye lids felt heavy, as though they were stuck together, and it took her a moment or two to process where she was.

"Hey," Gina said softly, and Lee heard the click of the kettle being switched on. "Sorry, I didn't mean to wake you. How are you feeling?"

Her mouth was too dry to answer immediately, and she didn't really know what the answer would be anyway. Slowly she sat up, feeling the room spin a little and grabbing a sip from the bottle of water that was on the coffee table.

"Not great," she answered truthfully. The room was quiet for a few minutes, until Gina wandered over with two mugs of tea and sat on the sofa opposite her.

"Sorry for sending James round - I was worried."

At the mention of his name, tears fell from Lee's eyes yet again and Gina rushed over to sit beside her on the sofa.

"Shit, what have I said? Lee, what's going on?"

"Oh Gina…" she said, feeling like she needed someone to help her make sense of everything that was going on in her life. "Everything just keeps being turned upside down. Just when I thought I had some sort of plan…"

"Lee, I don't get it. Did James do something? He seemed really worried when I rang him, if he's hurt you, I'll-"

"No, no, it's not his fault," Lee said, sniffing a little and taking a large gulp of tea. She proceeded to tell Gina about Lottie's appearance this morning, and her conversation with Val after.

"He hasn't… he hasn't left you to be with her has he?" Gina asked cautiously.

"No… I don't think so. I told him to go and sort out whatever he needed to - because I know what it's like to have someone from the past that you've had a whole lifetime with just turn up out of the blue and make everything more complicated. I'm not going to be that person who says he needs to just ignore her and focus on me."

"You're more mature about it than I would be…"

"It's killing me inside," Lee admitted, feeling that Gina wouldn't judge her. "But I'm trying. But… things have got even more complicated."

Gina didn't speak, and so Lee continued.

"I threw up before I made it home today. The owners of that sweet shop, you know, the one halfway up the hill? They made me go to the doctors. And… I'm pregnant."

"Well," Gina said, obviously at a loss for words. "I…I don't know what to say."

"Nor do I," Lee admitted. "Nor do I."

A glass of wine (for Gina) and a second cup of tea later, and Lee felt no closer to knowing what on earth to do with this news - but the tears had at least stopped.

"You've always wanted kids, right?" Gina asked, and Lee almost found it strange to think that she had a whole life and past that Gina had never known, had never been a part of. She was such an integral part of Lee's daily life now - but she had never known Nathan or her life with him back in Bristol.

"Yes. The time was never right... but yes, I always wanted to have kids. But that was when I had a plan, a house, a husband, a career..." She didn't want to insult Gina or what they had here, but things were different now. Things weren't as ordered, or as planned as she would have wanted when making this huge decision.

"And things with James are so new, and we said we were going to take things slowly - and this is the exact opposite of slow. And now with Lottie... I need to wait to see if he even wants to continue with this."

"Surely, once he knows you're pregnant, if you decide to go through with it-"

"I'm not going to tell him," Lee said, putting her mug down on the coffee table with more force than she intended. "Not until he has got his head together about Lottie. If I tell him, I'm fairly sure he will want to do the right thing - that's the kind of man I think he is. And I want him to decide about us based on us - not because I trap him with an unwanted pregnancy."

Privately, Gina didn't really agree with her plan - but now didn't seem like the right time to push that fact.

"So with James, you just have to wait, right?"

"Mmmhmm."

"But with this pregnancy - you can decide about that, can't you." It wasn't a question.

Lee considered that for a moment. A decision needed to be made, and it could be made - Gina was right. This decision needed to be made without knowing whether or not James was going to be a part of her life. She knew she was looking at a worst-case scenario, but she had to be realistic; she and James had only been seeing each other since December. The idea of a kid might freak him out. The reappearance of his ex might derail their relationship. He might simply decide that Lee wasn't the one for him... there were so many what ifs, and she knew that she needed to make this decision for herself. Because it may well be her alone dealing with whatever decision she made.

"Do you know what you want to do?"

"No... I don't know..." Lee took a deep breath. "I never thought I'd be in this position. I'm a planner - I always have been. And we've been careful..." She sighed, running a hand through her hair. "But yes, I do know. There's no way I could do anything else, I don't think, than continue with the pregnancy. Even if that does mean going it alone..."

Gina reached across and took hold of Lee's hand. "You won't be on your own, Lee. I promise you that."

Lee felt tears building in her eyes once more as she felt the safety of her friend's love.

Even though she knew sleep would evade her, Lee felt drained by the day's events and took herself off to bed after a long soak in a warm bath. Gina had told her to take a few days off, and while she knew the sickness would probably only get worse for a while, she was grateful to have a few days to regain her energy and make plans. She knew, to start with, that she needed some more permanence in her life - and that meant finally collecting her belongings from Bristol.

She pulled out her phone and sent a short, business-like message to Nathan's number, knowing that it was a necessary evil to move on to the next stage of her life.

I need to collect my things from the house. Will be there on Saturday at 12 - please be out.

The reply came moments later.

Okay.

Short and to the point. At the same time, another message popped up on the screen, one that filled her with a bubble of hope.

Hope you're feeling better - see you soon. J xxx

Lee awoke the next day - well, awoke was a bit of an

exaggeration, as there hadn't been much sleeping going on - determined to make a plan. Still in her pyjamas, with a cup of tea in one hand and a notebook in the other, she sat at the kitchen table in the empty flat and began to do what she did best: organise.

Make doctors' appointment. She had decided she was continuing with this pregnancy - now she needed to get on top of what that actually meant.

Collect belongings from Bristol. That was going to need something a bit bigger than her little car, she thought - even though she didn't really plan on bringing much in the way of furniture back with her. He was welcome to it; it held far too many bad memories anyway.

Talk to James. That was possibly the hardest of all - and something she knew needed timing right. He needed to have sorted out whatever was going on in his own head before she could burden him with all the things going on in hers.

Hire a new employee. The cafe was, she was pleased to note, going from strength to strength. Despite the post-Christmas nature of the month, they were doing well and actually making a profit. She and Gina needed to be able to have some time off - and, with a baby on the way, Lee needed someone she could rely on to support Gina. A new member of staff was definitely on the cards.

Speak to mum and Beth. Definitely one that was pushed further down the list... she didn't plan on telling any-one (besides Gina and, eventually, James) about this preg-nancy until she was past the twelve week mark - she'd done enough googling to know that was the sensible way to go about things. But that mark wasn't too far off, if the doctor had been right in her estimations, and she needed to prepare herself for the response the news would get. Not from Beth, really - but from her mother.

Without really realising she was doing it, she ran a hand backwards and forwards over her stomach. The sick feeling was definitely still there, but she was pleased to note that she hadn't actually thrown up yet that morning - although she also hadn't attempted any food yet. There was still time for that, though; she knew she needed to take care of herself. No drink, cut back on the caffeine, read up on all the foods she wasn't meant to eat... Even though it was terrifying, there was a bubble of excitement slowly building alongside that fear.

After a leisurely shower and a piece of dry toast that, thankfully, she'd managed to keep down, Lee took out her phone and tried to compose a message to James. As much as she didn't want to put any pressure on him if he was sorting his head out - or indeed having deep and meaningful conversations with Lottie (something that definitely made Lee want to throw up that toast), she also didn't want him to think she'd totally lost interest.

Heya - feeling a bit better today, thanks. Hope everything is okay with you - let me know when you want to meet. I'm off to Bristol on Saturday to pick up some things, but free other than that. Lee x She read back through it before sending, and hoped it wasn't putting any pressure on him to see her before he was ready, before hitting send.

A reply came back almost immediately. *So glad you're feeling a bit better. Want some company to Bristol? J xxx*

As tempting as it was, Lee felt this was something she needed to do without James. She wasn't sure she could cope with the mix of her old life and whatever her new life here might contain. And just imagine if Nathan ignored her wish to stay away...

I love that you offered, but think I need to do this on my own if that's okay? Xxx

Totally understand. How about I take you out Saturday night then? J xxx

Lee's heart soared and she smiled to herself.

Sounds perfect. Just let me know when. Xxx

She would see what he had to say about everything... and then maybe she could share everything that was going on for her.

Lee didn't feel any joy as she drove up the A38 and the M5 towards Bristol. She didn't need a sat nav; there was only one direction to travel in, until she reached Bristol itself. If felt odd to be heading away from Devon, and as she passed Exeter she was filled with memories of that night when she'd fled from Bristol with no real idea where she was going, or for how long - just that she needed to get away from the disaster that her life had turned into. She'd spent a night with her sister, Beth, on her way to Devon - and she wondered if she might have time today to stop off and have a catch up, before being back in Totnes for her seven o'clock date with James.

She very much hoped the queasiness would stay at that and not develop into full blown sickness today - else everything might take a lot longer.

Instead of her usual little car, she'd hired an estate (she had no idea what it was called, only that the boot was double the size of hers) and the journey was already a little slower due to her lack of confidence in the new vehicle. A longer journey was not what she needed - all the more time to mull over the reason she'd left Bristol in the first place.

Collecting the belongings that she still wanted from Bristol felt as though she truly was closing a door on her life there. She'd known when she'd made the decision to stay in Devon that things were changing, but visiting the house again for one last time was not going to be easy. It wasn't just morning sickness that fluttered in her belly as she approached the driveway; nerves were certainly playing a part in her nausea, she was sure.

There was no car on the drive, which Lee took as good sign. She presumed that, since she'd driven off with the only car they owned, he had bought a new one - and its absence hopefully meant he had complied with her request for him to be out. She knew she should be glad that he was on a decent salary - otherwise this separation and divorce would have been a lot more complicated.

The key slid into the lock just like it had done the previous year when it had been used on a daily basis, and for a second Lee had a strange sense of déjà vu, almost like nothing had changed.

Almost.

"Hello?" she called, not wanting to be surprised by anyone, but the house was blissfully silent.

She ran her hand lightly along the banister as she walked past it, feeling some sort of old connection with the place. Despite everything, this had been her home, and it almost felt like meeting an old friend after some sort of disagreement. Familiar, comfortable, but with a slight hint of unease breaking through the surface...

The house looked neat and tidy she thought, as she wandered into the kitchen that had been her pride and joy for so long, boxes in hand. She wondered if he'd hired a cleaner - or maybe there was a woman in his life who was taking care of the place for him. It hurt to think that, even though she knew full well that she didn't want to be the woman in his life any longer. She highly doubted he would have suddenly decided to keep on top of the housework; it wasn't something she had ever known him to do.

There wasn't much in the kitchen she wanted - a set of plates she had chosen, a few photographs and her favourite set of wine glasses that her mum had bought them for their wedding. She didn't feel she needed to ask permission to take any of this; it wasn't exactly valuable, and he was the one that had done the heart-breaking, after all.

The living room came next, and excluding a coffee mug on the table, it was pristinely tidy. It almost felt as though she had just stepped in from work and was about to settle down in front of the telly with a glass of wine. She found it hard to wrap her head around how much had changed in such a short space of time, and so she stopped bothering and focused on the task in hand. Some books, a few films and her blanket were the only items from this room - she knew most of what she wanted would be upstairs, in the room that had haunted her dreams, her nightmares, for so many weeks.

She ascended the stairs slowly, feeling her heart thudding as her feet touched each one, remembering that night so clearly. The strange feeling in the pit of her stomach at Nathan's lack of an answer when she'd shouted. That closed bedroom door...

It was closed now, and she half-expected to see the same sight as she pushed the door open gingerly. But no: the bed was made, there were no occupants this time, nothing that Lee wasn't supposed to see. She took a deep, shuddering breath and refocused her mind. The wardrobe. She slid the white wooden doors open to see all of her clothes hanging there, just like they had been back in November. Outfits that were her staples were now no longer really necessary - smart outfits for a barrister, not a barista. She hated the thought of Nathan just throwing them out, however, so she bundled them up into bags, not taking too much care to fold them - she wanted to be out of this place as quickly as she could. Her favourite linen sets and towels were thrown into bags too, and she emptied out the make-up and jewellery, thinking that whatever she no longer wanted she could always take to the charity shop. She thought she might need to, after surveying it all in the back of the car - there was no way all of this would fit in the room in the flat she shared with Gina.

After bundling everything into the car, she headed back into the house for one last look around. She didn't plan on coming back, and she wanted to make sure there was nothing she would miss - and to say goodbye one last time.

Her last sweep of the house only took a few minutes; she realised how few personal affects she'd really had there. It was in the kitchen, however, that she had a bit of a wobble. It was on the front of the fridge, pinned up with a magnet that she remembered placing there. A photo of the two of them in front of the sea at Weston-Super-Mare. They were laughing, arms slung around one another's backs, the sun setting behind them. She couldn't remember who had taken the photo, but she knew one thing - she had been happy then.

Was she happy now? She wasn't sure.

She shook her head to rid herself of the nostalgic tears that reminded her suddenly that she hadn't recovered from Nathan's betrayal as fully as she thought she had. Despite not being sure whether she was 100% happy, she knew one thing for sure: she wasn't miserable. And Nathan had made her miserable - in the end. A collection of happy times did not, unfortunately, make up for the bad.

She turned away from the sink and carefully spun the key off her keyring, deciding to leave it on the kitchen counter. She didn't need a key anymore; this was no longer her home. As she passed the bin, a whiff of what she presumed was the previous night's dinner made her stomach churn, and she only just realised in time that she was about to throw up. Emptying the contents of her stomach into that very same bin, Lee couldn't find it in herself to feel guilty. She couldn't help it, after all; it was the hormones.

A swig of water and a few deep breaths, and she was ready to leave. It took her a moment or two to be able to close the door behind her for that final time, and in her head she whispered goodbye. Goodbye to the house, goodbye to her life, goodbye to the past.

Now, she thought, as she drove away with one thumb swiping gently backwards and forwards over her stomach, was for the future.

CHAPTER SEVEN

The whole process had been thankfully simple - no interruptions from Nathan, which she had been concerned about - and her desire to get out of the house as quickly as possible meant that she was back on the road with time to spare. It was half four by the time she was close to Exeter, and without really thinking about it she turned off towards where her sister lived. There was always a chance that Beth would be out somewhere, but she didn't think her sister would mind an unexpected drop-in - and she didn't want to pass by so close and not pop in and say hi.

She hadn't decided, even as she pulled up outside her sister's house, whether or not she would tell Beth about the baby. On one hand, it seemed like a bad idea when James didn't know yet... On the other, Gina knew, and she could do with as much support as she could get. Inside her chest, she felt a little bubble of joy when she saw her sister's car outside and the lights on in the window, and she was pleased with the decision she'd made.

"Lee!" Beth exclaimed as soon as she opened the door. "Come in!"

"Sorry for just dropping by," Lee said, closing the door behind her and slipping her shoes off. "I had to go to Bristol and just thought I'd say hello."

"You know you're welcome any time, sis," Beth said, clicking the kettle on. "Coffee?"

Lee nodded. "Thanks."

"How are you doing? Sorry, I know I keep saying I'll come down to Totnes and then - well, things get crazy and I don't."

Lee laughed. "Don't worry, I know what it's like!" She glanced round the living room, marvelling at how different her state of mind was today than the last time she had been here. "Things... things are good," she said, wondering at how entirely true that statement was. Things seemed quite messed up... but she couldn't bring herself to feel too miserable about it all. That feeling that the world was falling down around her seemed to have calmed now... she just needed to discuss things with James. If everything could work out with him, then things would be really good.

"What were you doing in Bristol?" Beth asked, passing her a mug of coffee.

"Collecting my things... It was time."

Beth raised her eyebrows. "Wow. That's...final."

"It was already final, to be honest. The divorce is in progress, I've decided I'm staying in Devon for the foreseeable future - it's crazy for the stuff I want to be sat in Bristol, at risk of being chucked out or forgotten about."

"How are you feeling?"

"It was strange," Lee admitted. "Going back in there,

after everything. There were so many things I just didn't want anymore, now that everything's changed."

"And how's the gorgeous police officer?" Beth asked with a cheeky grin.

Lee smiled as she thought of James - despite the complications that were arising, the thought of seeing him this evening made her feel a little giddy. "He's good. Things between us... well, it's complicated. I hope it's all going to work out - I really hope it will. But if it doesn't, I won't regret it happening in the first place." She felt her eyes growing wet and blinked to try to hide it. Even though she meant every word, contemplating that things might not work out was a very painful prospect.

Beth reached out to squeeze her hand. "I'm sure things will work out."

Despite Beth not knowing the possible complications that lay in their path, Lee appreciated the gesture all the same. "Thanks, Beth."

After an hour of catching up on the news from their lives - minus one notable announcement - Lee said her goodbyes and headed down the A38 with promises to meet up very soon in either Totnes or Exeter. She knew she needed to get her head together before she saw James that evening. The fact that he wanted to take her on a date presumably suggested that he wasn't wanting to tell her he was still in love with Lottie and was running away with her or anything - but then she had been left reeling by a man's decisions before. Whatever he wanted to do, she knew she needed to tell him about the baby - but it had to be handled right. She was not going to use this pregnancy to make him commit if that was not what he wanted.

She was quite pleased to find the flat empty when she returned home, saving her from having to relay the details of her trip again quite so soon. She had managed to get herself into a fairly calm state as she drove, with an idea in her mind of the words she might use to drop this bombshell onto James. Luckily, she had the car until the following day and so wasn't in any rush to start emptying it out. In fact, she locked it and didn't remove a single box, instead choosing to change for her date. Without knowing where they were going, she picked a nice pair of black jeans, black ankle boots and a floaty long-sleeved top that shimmered a little in the light. She took her time over her make-up, wanting to look and feel good for a night that threatened to have her stomach tied in knots. It was as she was putting on a bold red lipstick that a wave of sickness hit her and she dashed to the kitchen in search of some plain food that might keep the feeling at bay. She had belatedly realised that she had forgotten to eat since breakfast - and that certainly wasn't going to help matters.

Dead on seven o'clock, the doorbell rang.

"Hey," he said, stood there in black jeans and a pale blue shirt that was open at the collar. His smile made Lee pause for a second, and as he leant in to kiss her she realised she had been assuming he would say goodbye, assuming that this wonderful experience was all going to be over.

He pulled away after a moment and looked slightly stunned to see tears in her eyes. "Hey, hey, what's the matter?"

"Nothing," Lee reassured him, delicately wiping the tears away with the corner of a tissue and taking his hand. "It's just been a long day."

It was a thirty minute drive to their destination, and on that journey they chatted about work, about Lee's visit to Bristol and about the weather - but not about Lottie, and definitely not about the pregnancy. The closest they got was James asking if she was definitely feeling better - she brushed this off without much of a response, not wanting to lie to him but also not wanting to get into that conversation in the car.

It had been dark for a while already and the winter's sky was an inky blue, peppered with stars and the flashing lights of a passing aeroplane. It seemed that both of them were keen to save any serious discussion until they were sat down and able to see each other face to face, and so they parked in fairly comfortable silence.

At the top of the sweeping driveway was a large building that Lee presumed was a hotel. It had floor-to-ceiling glass windows across most of the front of the building, looking out onto the bay - at least, she presumed that was the sea she could hear lapping gently beneath them. It was too dark to see properly, and James suddenly seemed to realise that as they approached the front door.

"I thought this would be a great spot because the views

are incredible... but I guess I didn't factor in that it would be dark."

Lee reassured him that it was still beautiful - and it was. As they were shown to a table in the hotel's restaurant, she could see the twinkling lights of a lighthouse and a few boats out on the water, and away from any real bright lights the stars were amazing to behold.

A single candle was lit on the table between them, and they were offered the wine list.

"I'll have a sparkling water, please," James said. "White, Lee?"

"No, just a lemonade please."

He waited until the waiter had left to query it. "Are you still not feeling great? You shouldn't have let me drag you out if you're still feeling rotten, I would have understood."

"No, no, I just don't fancy it," she said.

James took a deep breath, and reached forward to take one of her hands.

"I want to say sorry," he said, and Lee could feel nerves bubbling up inside her. "I shouldn't have just left the other day, after you told me you'd seen Lottie."

"I understand," Lee said. "You needed to clear your head. It makes sense."

"But it made it seem like any possibility with Lottie was more important than the relationship I have with you - and that's not the case. Not at all."

Lee smiled a little. "That's good to know."

"I went to see her - she was staying at her mum's, so not hard to find."

"You don't have to tell me, if you don't want to…"

"But I do want to. If you don't mind."

"I don't mind," Lee said softly. "I'm glad you want to share."

"I went round there, because I didn't want the idea of her hanging over everything in my life. She's visiting her mum, and considering moving back here for good." He swallowed, then took a drink from his glass of water that had arrived moments before. "She said she'd made a mistake - that we could start over again and make it work between us."

Lee felt as though she had been dunked into an ice cold pool of water. She couldn't quite breathe, and she couldn't quite think - she felt as though she was holding her breath, waiting for his response to this audacious request.

"And I told her that I've moved on, and that it wouldn't work. I told her I'm happy with someone else - and I'm sorry, because I know we said we were taking things slowly, that there was no real commitment - but Lee, I want to make decisions based on you. I want to commit to you. I don't want anyone else."

In a sudden rush, Lee let the breath go and felt as though she could laugh, or cry, or possibly a bit of both. "Are you sure?" she asked, hating herself for asking but knowing she had to. "That's a massive thing, being offered a chance to change history."

"History can't be changed, Lee. We'd be rehashing something that obviously didn't work - something I don't want anymore."

Lee squeezed his hand and found that words weren't that easy to come by.

"Are you ready to order?" The waited had returned, and Lee belatedly realised she hadn't even taken a look at the menu. She quickly scanned it for something plain that would be unlikely to trigger any sickness, and plumped for a tomato soup and a risotto.

"I don't want you to feel pressured, Lee. I'll stick by what we said, I promise - I won't rush you."

Lee took a deep breath in, closed her eyes for a second and then met his gaze with determination to share what was on her mind.

"The thing is, James, I'm not sure not rushing will be an option any more. Well, if..." Things were coming out a bit garbled, and she couldn't blame him for looking a little confused. "When I was ill, last week... I ended up going to the doctors. Well, the old woman who owns the sweet shop made me, after I was sick outside their shop." Not an image she particularly wanted James to have of her, she realised too late.

"I didn't know, Lee - I would have come and got you-"

"I know that, James - but here's the thing. I went to the doctors and - well. It wasn't a bug. I know this wasn't planned, and it's so much quicker than I could have ever imagined, and there is no pressure on you if this is all too much but - I'm pregnant."

"Pregnant?"

"About seven weeks," she confirmed.

"Pregnant." She didn't think it needed a response, and so she sat for a few minutes, letting him digest this monumental news.

When it had been silent for a little while, she felt compelled to speak again; "I've wanted a baby for a long time, James. Not that I planned this - god, that sounds awful. But I couldn't get rid of it - I just couldn't. And I would love to do this with you - but I know I'm thrusting a whole world, and a whole new life on you that you have no real say in, and I won't hate you if it's too much. I promise."

"It's just a lot to take in," James said, running a hand through his hair and trying to smile reassuringly. "I definitely wasn't expecting that..."

"Nor was I," Lee admitted. "The doctor had to repeat it several times."

"Well," he said. "Well." Another moment or two of silence, in which their soups arrived - but before Lee had chance to pick up her spoon, he seemed to have found the words he wanted to say.

"I'd never walk away, Lee. I hope you know that."

Lee smiled. "I didn't think you would."

"And it's sooner than I would have planned, granted - but I know I want to be with you. And having a baby with you - as terrifying as it sounds right now - will be a pretty amazing adventure. We can do this, can't we?"

"I don't think we have much choice!" Lee said with a laugh, and as he leant forward to kiss her, the words slipped out of her mouth without any thought, or planning, or consideration for their effect:

"I love you."

It seemed like they were the only two in the restaurant at that moment. Silence swam around them, the words almost hanging in the air between them, waiting for something...

"I love you too." There it was; what they had both been waiting for. The words seemed to flow easily from James' lips, joining Lee's words and surrounding them. Had Lee considered where she would be in February back in November when her life had tumbled from her grasp, this would never have entered her wildest dreams. Hell, had she considered last week that she would be pregnant and telling James she loved him, she wouldn't have believed it.

She blushed a little at his words, at his intense gaze, but she didn't break eye contact. James laughed, and took a sip of his water. "We didn't do taking things slow and casual very well, did we?" he said.

Suddenly realising how hungry she was, Lee began to eat her soup. "I'm not sure I can really do casual - despite it being my idea!"

"I'm glad."

They ate for a few moments, digesting the news of the day without really talking. As their plates were cleared away, Lee couldn't help but ask a question of him.

"Are you scared?"

"Of not going slowly and casually?"

Lee shook her head. "Of having a baby."

James shrugged. "It seems a little surreal, to be honest. I mean, we were careful, it wasn't exactly something I was expecting…"

"Me neither," Lee jumped in, keen to assure him that this was not some master plan. "I think maybe we weren't so careful that night… when we'd had a lot to drink…"

"You're probably right," James said, raking a hand through his hair. "Are you scared?"

"Terrified," Lee admitted. "It's not exactly how I'd planned it… when I thought about how my life would pan out."

"I'm sorry things haven't gone how you wanted."

"No! No, I didn't mean it like that. Now that I know you're on board… I'm terrified because it's all so sudden. But I'm really excited, too."

James grinned. "Talk about life-changing news," he said.

"Never a dull moment!"

"Not since I met you."

CHAPTER EIGHT

They arrived back at James' under a blanket of fog, and Lee was pleased James was driving. Whilst she was getting used to the winding roads and small lanes, driving them in the dark and fog was a bit more of a challenge than she fancied. In front of the fire place with mugs of tea, they began to talk of practicalities.

"So... seven weeks. When would that make you due?"

"Sometime in October, I think. My dates are a bit erratic, so I don't think they'll know until they've done the scan."

"I feel like I need to spend several hours on the internet, getting my head around everything that's going to happen."

"Me too," Lee agreed. "I'm no expert - I may have wanted a baby but I've not got any actual experience." She leaned back against James, who was propped up against the sofa. "What if I'm terrible at it?"

His fingers kneaded the small of her back in a way that made her drift off into a much calmer place. "You won't be," he said. "I'm sure of it."

"I wish I had your confidence," she said with a sigh.

"My mother... I love her, but things have always been a little strained between us. A little formal. Not like you and your mum..."

"Have you told your mum yet?" James asked, and Lee shook her head.

"I wasn't going to tell anyone until I'd told you..."

"But...?"

"How did you know there was a but?"

"I could sense it," he said with a short laugh.

"Gina was worried, I was in a bit of a state. I'm sorry I told her first."

His fingers moved up her spine, slowly pressing into the tired flesh around her back bone. "It's okay."

"I'm so pleased you're okay with this," she said, closing her eyes and letting the sensation of his impromptu massage take over. "I had talked myself into letting you go... that you wanted to be with Lottie, that you wouldn't want to take on me and a baby... I'm just so glad I was wrong."

The massaging stopped, and before she knew it she was no longer lying against James but next to him on the rug in front of the fire. "Lee," he said, fixing her eyes with his. "I'm really sorry I made you feel like that."

"You didn't-" she tried to interrupt, but he didn't let her.

"You are the most important thing to me. You, and now our baby. I'm ready for this, I promise you. I'm ready for this step in my life. I love you."

It was the most glorious thing Lee thought she had ever heard. She moved herself closer to him, entwining her arms around his body so that they were so wrapped up in one another they were almost one. "I love you James. I love you."

It wasn't until the wee hours of the morning, when Lee shivered a little and stretched an aching arm, that they realised that they had fallen asleep entwined on that rug in front of the fire, and that the fire was now most definitely dead.

"James..." Lee whispered. "James, let's go to bed."

He grunted a little at her prodding, and when he eventually opened his eyes he looked more than a little confused.

"We fell asleep," Lee said. "Come on, let's go to bed."

"There's an offer I'd never turn down."

Lee laughed softly, as hand-in-hand they padded across the carpet through the dark hallway to James' bedroom.

James stifled a yawn. "You don't have to be up early tomorrow - I mean this morning, do you?"

Lee shook her head. "Cafe's closed. How about you?"

"Day off," he said with a grin. He pulled her hand to stop her from walking forwards, and ran a hand through her blond locks. She closed her eyes at the sensation.

"How are you feeling?" he asked.

"Amazing."

He didn't need any further prompting. His lips were on hers in a physical display of that love they had confessed only hours earlier. Her hands wound around his waist, and the electricity between them, if possible, took on an even more intense quality. The room around them seemed to crackle with tension as Lee removed James' top, and then her own.

Right now they didn't need words - they could show each other the insane strength of those feelings without them.

The next time they woke up was in a little more comfort; winter sunshine was streaming through the windows and they were together under the heavy down duvet. It was James who woke first this time, but he lay for quite a while with Lee curled up in his arms, staring up at the ceiling and contemplating this huge change in his life.

When he felt Lee beginning to stir next to him he slipped carefully from the bed and into the kitchen, where the cold tiles made him regret not pausing for slippers. The filter coffee was drizzling out into the pot in no time, and when he reappeared in the bedroom with two steaming mugs of coffee, he was greeted by a sleepy grin from Lee.

"I was worried you'd run off," she said, only half-joking.

"In my own house?" James laughed. "Can't get rid of me

that easily I'm afraid."

Lee took a big swig from the mug, holding it carefully in two hands, then looked down at it again. "I guess I really should be limiting how much caffeine I'm having," she said with a sigh. "There's so much I need to look into."

"You'll already know more than me, I can promise you that," James said. He rubbed her knee with the palm of his hand; "Try not to panic. We can do this, I'm sure of it."

Lee smiled at his confidence in their abilities, and nodded. The worries certainly hadn't disappeared, but she knew many of them were irrational.

"When should we tell people?" James asked.

None of this quite seemed real; sat in a t-shirt and knickers in her boyfriend's bed, casually discussing announcing their pregnancy. "It's fairly standard to not tell anyone until after the twelve-week scan," she said, realising there were some things she knew. "That's when the risks have dropped off a bit."

"So you want to wait 'til then?"

"I think so, yeah, if you don't mind. It's only five weeks...maybe less, if my dates were not accurate."

"Yeah, that's fine, I just can't wait to tell my mum - she's going to be thrilled, I know it."

Lee grinned at his excitement, despite being fairly sure that her own mother was not going to be thrilled. It wasn't about being a grandmother - it was about Lee deviating from the life plan. And deviate she most certainly had done - although, to be fair, the catalyst to that deviation had not been her fault.

Since the previous night's date by the sea had not really showcased the ocean, they decided to head out - once they had eaten a leisurely breakfast and showered - on the sunny, blustery Sunday towards Paignton, and some golden sands they could sink their toes into. The wind was biting cold but the sun streamed out in front of them and, wrapped up in coats, scarves, gloves and a bobble hat for Lee, it wasn't too uncomfortable.

"I still get a rush of excitement, every time I come to a beach," Lee said, holding James' hand as they stepped onto the sand. Despite the cold, Lee had insisted on at least briefly removing her shoes so she could feel the sand properly.

"I forget you didn't grow up near beaches!" James said with a laugh. "I mean, I love it, but I guess I take it for granted - I've pretty much always been able to go to the beach whenever I liked."

"Lucky for some!"

"I meant to ask more," James said after a few minutes, "But the news last night kind of derailed me. Did you get everything sorted in Bristol?"

Lee nodded - "I've got to return the car I borrowed today, and get all my stuff out of it. I kind of abandoned it all last night when I got back."

"We can do that this afternoon, if you like," James said.

"Thank you. But yeah, I got everything I needed. It was a bit... strange. Like stepping back into some vision of the past, but feeling like you don't really belong anymore. But I'm glad I did it - I needed to close the door on my life then."

James gave her hand a squeeze. "Nathan didn't show up, then?"

"No," Lee said with a shake of her head. "Thank god."

She wondered if he'd been concerned about her seeing him; she knew that things were over between them, but then equally she knew how she'd felt about him seeing Lottie. Jealousy certainly wasn't always logical, or rational.

"Do I get to meet your mum, and your sister then?" James asked, and for a moment Lee was taken aback by the question. She hadn't really imagined her mum meeting James - but then she guessed it was an inevitability now.

"Yeah, I guess - once we've told them all. I can't promise my mum will be nice..."

"I'm good at charming mothers," he said with a grin that she couldn't deny she found charming. "Plus, I'm a police officer. Generally fairly high up in what mothers want for their daughters, no?"

"You haven't met mine!" she said with a laugh. "She'll be more likely to see you as a handsome rogue who sidetracked her daughter from whatever the life plan should have been!"

Far from looking offended, James' eyes seemed to sparkle in the sunlight with humour. "Handsome rogue... I quite like that description!"

Lee swiped at his arm. "You would! What about your family? Will you introduce me as your girlfriend?"

"Ah, Lee. I think they knew I was smitten with you before I'd even admitted it, I'm afraid to say. The fact that we would end up together has been a foregone conclusion in the Knight household for quite some time."

Lee felt a warm glow at the thought of his warm family accepting her into the fold. "And they won't see me as some older woman, leading their son astray, saddling him with a child?"

"Are you kidding? They'll be thrilled. Grandchildren are high on their list of priorities - and they thought I was a lost cause in that department, what with my single status for so long."

"You mean you hadn't previously had a nutty potential girlfriend turn up on your doorstep and hijack your family Christmas dinner before? I'm shocked." Lee giggled.

"I mean that, aside from Lottie, there's not really been anyone. And since her... there's been no-one. I didn't think... I thought I was broken. I thought I couldn't do this again." He paused and she stopped next to him, her hair whipping around her face, the sunlight making her squint a little.

"I know how fast this all seems, but I want you to know I'm all in - I didn't think I could feel safe with someone again until I met you. I didn't think I would fall in love like this - and I have. My parents will be overjoyed because they know I've found the one."

Lee was taken aback. It wasn't the response she'd expected to her gentle ribbing, and his sincerity silenced her momentarily. She blinked in the sunlight, seeing the light bounce off his piercing blue eyes, with the sea in the background that was almost the exact same colour. She didn't know whether it was the hormones, or just an emotional response to him laying himself so bare to her, but the words began to tumble from her mouth.

"I thought there was something wrong with me. I thought that for him to cheat like that, I must be broken. Damaged. Unloveable. And I was so convinced I would be on my own for a long time to heal, and to figure out where I'd gone wrong, and to fix whatever it was. And then you looked at me like I was special, and now I think I've realised that I didn't do anything wrong - that there is no excuse. That it wasn't my fault. And even if the timeline has gone up the creek, there isn't anyone else I'd want to do this with."

A kiss seemed like the only way to mark such momentous declarations, and there in the middle of the beach, with only a few dogs and their owners as witnesses, James Knight and Lee Davis pressed their lips together in a timeless symbol of love, of unity, of understanding.

"Let's invite them down for an Easter lunch," James suggested as they strolled daringly close to the sea, occasionally having to hop back to avoid getting wet feet. "Then we can tell them all at the same."

"And by them all you mean…" Lee raised her eyebrows.

"Your mum, sister, my parents and siblings…"

"For Easter lunch? Where?"

"Mine? I've got the space, and you know I'm happy to cook. Look, you seem a bit worried about how your mum will take it, but if my mum and dad are ecstatic then I bet it will change your mum's reaction."

"I wouldn't bet on it…" Lee said, but she was grinning anyway. "Okay. Let's do it. They're going to be suspicious at me inviting them down as it is - but at least we can announce it to everyone all at once. Then it'll properly seem real…"

CHAPTER NINE

Back at Lee and Gina's flat, with rosy cheeks and wind swept hair, Lee and James contemplated the collection of items in the estate car.

"Not much to show for an entire adult life so far, is it," Lee said.

James squeezed her hand. "You've started again - that's nothing to be ashamed of. Besides, there's no point dragging a load of things with you that you don't want any more."

"No," Lee agreed. "Better to start fresh."

As they began to unload, James refused to let Lee carry anything that looked remotely heavy, and so ended up taking most of the things up to Lee's room by himself. Carrying a cushion that she had been allowed to bring upstairs, she surveyed her now rather packed room.

"Hmm. It didn't look so much in the house, or in the car..."

"I guess some of it can go around the house?" James suggested. "I mean, I've put everything here for now but some of it looks like it could be kitchen stuff, or round the living room maybe?"

"Yeah, I guess."

"There'll be more stuff soon," James said with a slight raise of his eyebrows. "From what I've heard, babies need a lot of stuff."

"Yeah…" Lee sat down on the edge of the bed, feeling a slight dizziness that she wasn't sure was entirely pregnancy related. "I guess I hadn't thought… I'm going to need to find somewhere to live. I mean, I can't exactly have a baby in one bedroom of a shared flat. That's hardly going to be fair on Gina. Although, until the divorce is finalised, I certainly won't have the capital to buy somewhere…"

"Or…" James began, and Lee looked up.

"Or?"

"Or…you could move in with me?"

"Move in with you?"

"Yeah. I mean…" James shrugged. "We're having a baby together. We love each other. It seems to make sense, to me, that we live together, that we raise the baby together. I mean, otherwise, what are we going to do? Have two sets of everything? Stay in each other's places, taking the baby between each?" James gave her that intense look where it felt as though his blue eyes could see straight into her deepest, darkest thoughts - but when she hadn't responded after a few seconds, the intensity faded a little. "What do you think?"

"I think…" Lee responded slowly. "I think that I haven't thought any of this through. And I think that I'm going to be sick if I don't eat something right away."

"Sit tight, I'll grab you something."

"Something very plain!" Lee shouted from the bedroom, taking a few deep breaths to try to abate the sickness that her sudden hunger was threatening to bring about.

In two shakes of a lamb's tail, James was back with a hastily made cheese sandwich and a packet of ready salted crisps. He perched on the bed too and Lee leant back against him, feeling reassured by his presence as she nibbled on the cheese sandwich and, thankfully, felt the sickness subside.

"That's a massive step that you're talking about," she said between mouthfuls.

"Bigger than having a baby?"

That threw her for a moment, and she ate a handful of crisps to fill the silence. "Okay, maybe it's not bigger than that, but it's different. It's a choice. It's a life plan. And... and I don't want a big decision like that to be made because it would be practical. I want it to be because it's the right thing for us - because it's what we really want."

"It would be practical," James countered. "And it is what I really want." She felt him press a kiss into the curve of her neck and closed her eyes briefly.

"Can I have some time to think about it?" she asked, knowing that she was in danger of just saying yes because it would be easy, and it would make him happy, and it really did sound like a wonderful picture - James, her and a little baby in that beautiful house, having lunch in the kitchen or lying by the fire in the winter. But she didn't want to be seduced by his smile or the fanciful images that were already populating in her mind. She wanted to be rational about this, to decide based on her feelings after careful consideration.

"Of course. I'm not trying to rush you, I promise. It just hit me as the perfect solution."

"And I love that you want to... I just need to think things through, okay?"

"Absolutely. Feeling better?"

"So much better. It's amazing how hunger and sickness can be so intertwined!"

James was working a night shift that evening and so after helping Lee try to rearrange all of her belongings so that she could actually make her way to her bed to sleep that night, he left Lee to enjoy a cup of tea in the bath which went a long way to soothing her aching muscles after the trials of driving, packing, unpacking, walking — all in all a busy couple of days.

She heard the front door opening just as she was getting out of the bath, and shouted in response to Gina's call: "In the bathroom! Two minutes!"

She wrapped herself in one of the teal towels she had brought back from Bristol with her, and revelled in how soft it was on her skin. She dressed slowly, mindful that the heat of the bath had the potential to exacerbate her dizziness, and once she was in her comfy pyjamas and fluffy dressing gown, she opened the door to find Gina looking irritated.

"What's up?" Lee asked, concerned - Gina was not usually one to get annoyed over nothing.

"Just had a frustrating Sunday lunch with my parents, that's all," Gina said, rolling her eyes and running a hand through her purple-tipped hair. "Anyway, your news is way more important. I presume you were at James' last night, since you weren't here? Did you tell him?"

Lee sunk onto the sofa next to Gina. "Yeah, I did. And... and he's been amazing. He was shocked, but he wants to do this together - oh, Gee, he even asked me to move in with him!"

Gina looked stunned. "To move in with him?"

"Yeah. When I said that I didn't know where everything was going to fit, and how I can't exactly keep living here once I've had this baby, he asked me. I mean, I said I'd have to think about it, but the fact that he wants to-"

"When was it decided that you couldn't live here after the baby is born?" Gina asked, a slight edge to her voice that Lee didn't think she'd ever heard before.

"I just thought - I mean, you don't want - Gina, I-" Her mindless babble was cut off by Gina standing up and turning to look down at Lee.

"Maybe you should have asked me what I wanted, before just assuming." And with that she walked into her bedroom and closed the door. It wasn't quite a slam, but Lee got the message.

For a few moments, Lee sat and stared at the door Gina had disappeared through. It was like she couldn't quite comprehend what had just happened; she had known Gina was in a bad mood, so perhaps that was it.

A few more moments, and it began to dawn on Lee how insensitive she had been. Moving out would, of course, be a massive change in Gina's life - and Lee realised she had very definitely been viewing it from her own point of view alone.

She moved towards the door, and took a deep breath before knocking. "Gina? Gina, can I come in?"

There was a noise of some sort from the other side of the door, and Lee took it to mean she could go ahead. When she entered, Gina was curled up on the bed, on top of the black and white spotted duvet cover, and the lights hadn't been switched on.

Gina didn't look up, not even when Lee sat on the bed.

"Gina... I'm really sorry. That was a really insensitive thing to just blurt out, and I'm so sorry."

For a tense minute, Lee didn't think Gina was going to respond. She let out a quiet sigh of relief when her friend rolled over and faced her. Although the room was dark, enough light was coming in from the living room to show Lee that Gina had been crying.

"I'm really sorry, Gina," she repeated, feeling terrible that her words had caused so much pain.

"It's okay," Gina said quietly. "I know you didn't mean to be an insensitive bitch." There was a half-smile there, and Lee took it as a good sign.

"I really didn't," she said. "I'm just completely thoughtless."

"And... it's not just you. I've had a crappy day all round, so this was just the icing on the cake, really."

"What happened?"

Gina pulled herself up so she was sitting and leant over to flick the switch on her bedside lamp. "I had Sunday lunch with my parents, and a couple of aunts and uncles," she said. "And, as usual, it starts down the route of 'why don't you have a boyfriend yet?' and 'When will you settle down and live an adult life?'" Gina sighed and shook her head. "What part of helping run a cafe and paying rent and bills isn't living an adult life, I don't know. Anyway— my dad starts joking that at least I've moved on from my 'phase' of dating women."

Lee could feel her eyes widening slightly - this was news to her.

"You knew I was bi, right? No, I guess not. Well, I am, but I haven't dated a woman in a couple of years so obviously it was a phase and it's perfectly acceptable to joke about 'silly little Gina' and how she 'just needs to settle down with a good man'. I swear he's from the middle ages." Gina took a deep breath, her first in a while, and continued. "And then I get home and you're talking about moving out. It was just the last straw - and I'm sorry for going a bit mental at you."

"No, it's not something I should have just said like that. It's not even something that's agreed - I was as shocked when he said it as you were. And I'm sorry you're having a crappy time with your parents. I would say that - even though I know from experience that it doesn't make it any easier - they probably do mean it from a good place — they just don't know how to show it."

"I know they're not evil or anything," Gina said with a bit of a sniff. "But to be laughed at like that in front of everybody... I can only assume they don't know how much it hurts."

Lee laid a hand on Gina's. "I bet they don't. Again, it's a lot easier to say when it's not you, but maybe talk to them in private when you're calm, and let them know how it makes you feel. You never know, they might lay off."

Gina shrugged. "You're probably right. Anyway, I'm really pleased that James is on board with everything. I always thought he would be - seems like he's one of the good ones."

Lee couldn't help but smile. "Yeah, I think you're right."

CHAPTER TEN

"I need your help." It was ten o'clock on Monday morning, and Lee had to admit she had been daydreaming a little while nibbling on a cracker - something she found was handy for keeping the sickness away - when Shelley approached the counter. While she didn't know Shelley particularly well, her job as the receptionist at the doctors' surgery meant she had spoken to her on a handful of occasions now - and, of course, she had thrown up outside Shelley's grandparents business. Not the sort of thing that was easily forgotten.

"What can I do for you?" Lee asked, brushing off a few stray crumbs from her apron and trying to avoid showing her surprise at the blunt request.

"I'm pregnant," Shelley announced, seemingly unconcerned by the fact that the whole cafe could hear her. "And my job - not the doctors, I work in a bar in the evenings - have conveniently decided that my services are no longer required. Anyway, I heard you were a lawyer and could help me out."

"Well, I was a lawyer - back in Bristol." It was only a few short months ago, she mused, that she had been in court picking apart complex custody cases or acrimonious divorces. While this certainly wasn't her area of law expertise, it sounded like a fairly cut and dried situation - if Shelley was telling her all the facts. "But I'm happy to help, if you want me to."

"That'd be amazing. I can't afford to pay for anyone right now..."

"That's fine. Come back after I close up, we can discuss the details, okay?"

Shelley left looking happier than she had when she entered, and Lee felt a little thrill that she didn't quite understand. Was it happiness at being able to help someone? Or at being involved in some sort of law dispute, however minor?

She decided to contemplate that later, when she wasn't faced with a sudden line of customers wanting coffees and cakes.

At five-thirty, Shelley reappeared with a few loose sheets of paper and Lee provided the coffees. They sat at a small, round table that Lee had recently wiped clean of coffee spills and cake crumbs.

"So," Lee said. "Tell me what happened."

And so Shelley filled her in on her time at the bar and her contract, with a healthy dose of colleague gossip weaved in between. Lee took copious notes, scrutinised the slightly mussed pieces of paper Shelley had brought to her and asked questions - when she could get a word in edge-ways.

"What do you think?" Shelley finally asked as she got to the end of her appeal.

"I think... I think it's wrongful termination. I think they thought they could get away with it, that you wouldn't realise, that they didn't want the hassle of dealing with finding someone to cover you - but they can't do that. They can't hire women and just get rid of them because they're pregnant."

"So what do I do?"

"I'll send them a letter, explaining your rights and why they're in the wrong. I would imagine that'll be enough - the idea of being sued for wrongful termination will terrify them."

Shelley grinned. "Thank you so much, Lee, I really appreciate it."

Lee wondered if Shelley knew about her pregnancy; she guessed that she probably did, but she also knew that her notes were confidential, and if Shelley let on about that she would be looking at termination from that job - rightfully, this time. Lee wasn't ready to share the news herself yet - not before they'd told their families, certainly - and so she didn't confide that this case was more personal to her than it may have seemed.

"No problem. If I can keep these documents for now, I'll get something drafted up and sent over to them tomorrow, and get them back to you."

Without a printer, it would prove slightly trickier than it would have done in her office back in Bristol, but as she said goodbye to Shelley and locked up she was already thinking of a plan to go and use the one in the library... or perhaps see if James owned one. It seemed likely - he had a decent sized house, and a little room that he referred to as the office. Not that she'd ever really looked in there, but it would seem quite standard to have a printer. That was something she could have brought with her from the house in Bristol - something she hadn't really considered needing. Business with the cafe was all quite small-scale; handwritten notes or emails had sufficed so far.

As she mindlessly performed the end of day tasks - checking the doors and windows were locked, sockets were switched off, nothing was going to set the place on fire - she began to contemplate James' house. That perfect little cottage, with its exposed wooden beams and real fireplace. The gorgeous marble kitchen, three bedrooms, one of which she was sure would be a perfect nursery... her hand found its way to rest on her stomach without even thinking about it, and she found herself picturing the three of them in that house. It did make sense, he was right... they could raise the baby together, properly, rather than some strange version of co-parenting that was usually the domain of separated parents, not ones embarking on a new life together. They could share the challenges that a baby was bound to bring - and the joys.

But then... was it all too soon? She wondered if she were dooming this relationship, putting it to the test by living together and having a baby in such a short amount of time.

But if not now, when? When the baby was born? When it was six months, a year? None of this was how she'd planned - and she couldn't see any perfect timing for any of it.

And he loved her. And she loved him.

As she exited the building and triple-checked the lock, she suddenly saw him unexpectedly waiting there for her, pulled up outside the building in his car. Her heart danced in her chest like a ballerina on the verge of taking flight; her smile was impossible to control. She loved him - and he loved her.

She flung the door open and climbed in, not bothering to do up her seatbelt before turning to kiss him.

"Well, hello to you too!" he said with a smile as wide as hers. "Good day?"

"Yeah, actually. And I've been thinking about it all day - I think you're right. I think we should move in together before this baby is born."

"I think you're right. Today?"

"Whoa, hold your horses." Lee laughed. "This baby isn't being born any time soon. I need time to adjust to the idea, and to get Gina prepared for it and probably find her a new flat mate. But once we buy stuff - we'll just buy one set. Because we're doing this together."

He took her hand and kissed the knuckles. "One hundred percent."

CHAPTER ELEVEN

It was a wet and windy March day, and Lee knew she would remember it for the rest of her life. She wrapped up warm and chose to drive down the hill to work, parking in the car park around the corner and then battling against the wind to get to the front door of Carol's Cafe. She felt exhausted from the effort of combatting with the elements by the time she'd got through the door, and the business of the day ahead seemed impossible to contemplate.

First, there was opening up. She was doing fewer of the early starts since the further her pregnancy progressed, the more exhausted she seemed to become - but it didn't seem to be fair to get Gina to do all the early ones, even though she had offered. Then at ten, once Gina had hopefully arrived, they were due to interview a couple of candidates to take up some of the slack that Lee was causing - and give them both a break when they needed it. And then - the biggest event of the day - James was picking her up at four so they could go to the twelve week scan and see their little baby for the first time. Every time she thought about it, Lee felt a bubble of excitement, a hint of panic and a fervent hope that everything would be okay.

The morning's tasks were relatively simple, something Lee was grateful for since she was struggling to keep her mind on the job. It wasn't just because of the scan, although that was certainly a large part of it. No, there was also a niggling feeling that she'd had for a little while now, that wouldn't quite go away. A desire to research, and to argue a case, and to win. That conversation with Shelley had only stoked the fire - and now she found her mind wandering to the idea whenever she wasn't busy - and sometimes when she was. She'd equated being a lawyer with her old life, with Bristol, with living in Clifton and working in that office. She'd thought it had no place in this new life she was beginning - but she was starting to wonder if she'd been wrong about that.

She turned the sign to 'open' and caught sign of the ad in her handwriting that she'd placed there a couple of weeks ago, alongside matching ones in the newsagents and on the local news board in the town square.

Wanted: responsible, flexible person to complete cafe duties including making and serving coffees and cakes, working a till and cashing up. Experience desirable but not essential.

There had been a flurry of replies, and they had chosen the two most promising to interview that day. The hours would need to be flexible, and the ideal person needed to be willing to cover all of Lee's hours once she was on maternity leave - but she was getting ahead of herself. First they needed to meet the two people and see whether either of them felt like a good fit.

By nine, Gina had breezed through the door and laughed at Lee's surprise.

"I wanted to get ahead of things!" she said. "With interviews at ten. I thought I'd get in a bit earlier and bake a batch of scones, if you're all right on your own out here."

Lee surveyed the cafe; three tables had customers, but she could certainly cope without any help. "Go ahead - we've only got three scones left, so I was going to do it after lunch if I had time anyway."

"Great minds," Gina said with a laugh, scraping her hair into a messy bun and throwing an apron on before washing her hands.

"What if we get a mad rush in the interviews?"

"I'll serve, you interview," Gina said. "You'll be better at that anyway. Just let me have a quick word before you hire anyone, please, so I can make sure they aren't going to drive me mental!"

"Of course, we both have to sign off on them. No question about that."

It was five past ten by the time the first candidate showed up - soaked through and carrying an inside-out umbrella. He was just shy of six foot, with brown hair and a red rain coat.

"I'm so sorry," he said, the second he'd stepped foot through the door. "The bus got delayed, and then the rain started bucketing down - anyway, I'm so sorry I'm late, and looking like this." He gestured to his drowned-rat image, then held out his hand to shake Lee's and Gina's.

Lee smiled to herself. This situation was not unfamiliar to her - it reminded her very much of the horrendous day on which, among other things, she'd found out that Nathan was having the affair with the blonde. In fact, the nature of his late arrival rather warmed her to the twenty-three-year-old before her.

"No problem. Come, take a seat, can I get you a coffee? Tea?"

While he took off his wet coat and abandoned his almost certainly ruined umbrella, Gina made him a tea - with milk, no sugar, 'however it comes'. Handily - although not for their till balance - the cafe currently only boasted one customer, and so both Lee and Gina took a seat at the four-person table in the corner of the room, opposite the one the young man had occupied.

"So, it's Tom, isn't it?"

"Yeah, Tom Dent."

"Great. So, I'm Lee Davis, I'm the owner and co-manager, and this is Gina Travis, the other manager. First of all, let me make it clear what we're looking for: at the minute we do all the hours, but that's not sustainable. We're looking for someone to do a couple of days a week, but ideally to be able to do more days if either of us needs any time off." Lee wasn't ready just yet to announce her pregnancy to anyone. Even though she didn't know Tom, or any Dents, in a town as small as this there was a very good chance he would know someone she did - or be related to them, most likely. It was the way things seemed to go.

"That sounds brilliant. I'm a freelance journalist and, while I love it, it doesn't exactly pay regularly. So I'm really looking for something that I can do alongside that - but the positive to that is that if there's more hours, I'll definitely be available to take them on."

Lee smiled. "So I can put a tick next to flexibility then. Can you tell us why you want to work here?"

At that moment, another rain-soaked customer entered, and Gina muttered her apologies and jumped up to serve them.

"I've worked in cafes before," Tom said, "And I've been trained as a barista, so it seemed like a natural choice to go for a cafe. I've walked past here plenty of times and it always looks busy, and from what I've heard there's lots of repeat customers, which sounds great because I like getting to know people."

Lee nodded, and made a couple of quick notes on her pad.

"And do you have any questions about working here?"

"I don't think so - I mean, I think you answered everything at the beginning."

"Okay. Last thing then - what jobs have you done previously, other than journalism?"

Tom reeled off cafe work when he was a teenager, a stint at the university magazine and a couple of bar jobs, doing a good job of linking them to skills he could use in the cafe. Although she needed Gina to sign off, Lee definitely felt that he ticked all the right boxes.

Gina reappeared just as Lee had run out of things to ask - it seemed that there wasn't an awful lot she needed to know about someone to work in the cafe - just that she liked them, and that they knew what they were doing.

"Well, I think I've got everything I need. Gina, have you got anything else you'd like to ask?"

Gina glanced over at her notes, and shook her head.

"Nope, all sounds good. Thanks for coming in, Tom - we'll be in touch later today if that's okay."

"Thank you - and sorry again for being late. And thanks for the amazing coffee!"

Lee laughed. "Flattery will get you far!"

The second interviewee - a woman also in her early twenties - although nice, did not feel like the right fit for them. She had two other jobs, and so didn't have the flexibility, nor Tom's barista experience. Plus she just didn't click the same way he did - it was a gut feeling decision, but one Gina and Lee both agreed on.

At midday, Lee let Gina ring Tom and give him the good news. They arranged for him to come in the next day for a training and getting-to-know-you session, and then go from there. Lee felt a rush of excitement; things were moving on. This plan for the future - running the cafe, but not necessarily being in there every day in the early hours - was beginning to be set in motion.

It was at twelve-thirty that it happened; Lee remembered because she'd looked up at the clock only seconds before and noticed that it was already half past the hour, and that there weren't too many hours to go until she could pack up and be ready to meet James outside for their exciting appointment.

"Have you heard?" A short brunette woman rushed through the door, making the bell chime as she raced in to join a load of her friends at the counter. They were about eighteen or so, Lee thought, and they were becoming fairly regular now, coming in as a group at least once or twice a week.

"Heard what?" one of the friends replied, as Lee wandered over from where she had been wiping down tables to take the girl's order.

"There's some sort of hostage situation at that betting shop - the one up the hill, on that little street to the left."

"A hostage situation? In Totnes? You're talking nonsense," a ginger boy wearing a bright red scarf piped up.

"I know, but it's true. Some guy got angry in there apparently, pulled a knife, and started threating the staff and customers saying he wanted money."

Lee couldn't help but interrupt. Her face felt as white as milk and a wave of nausea and dizziness came over her that, for once, she didn't think was baby-related. "Are the police there?"

The girl looked quite pleased to have gathered a crowd - or at least, an extra spectator - and did not look surprised at Lee's rude interruption.

"Oh yes - two cars with blaring sirens and flashing lights had arrived on the scene. Apparently one of the police officers was in there, trying to calm the guy down, but no-one else had managed to get in or out."

Fumbling for the stool that she knew was behind the counter, Lee felt the need to sit down as quickly as was possible.

Gina noticed - of course she did - and was straight over, cutting short the chat she'd been having with a local.

"Lee?" she asked. "Lee? What's up, are you feeling sick? Dizzy?"

Both of those were true - but they weren't the issue. She took a deep breath to calm her heart, which had begun racing without her permission. "There's some guy… with a knife, in the bookies up the road. The police are there, and one of them is in the building, trying to talk the guy down…"

Lee felt an overwhelming urge to throw up, and rushed to the kitchen behind the counter where the customers couldn't see her - and she hoped, couldn't hear her - throw up into a bucket.

"Is she all right?" she heard one of the group ask Gina.

"She'll be okay," Gina replied. "Her boyfriend's in the police, but I'm sure everything will be okay." She said that for Lee's benefit more than the girl's, who shrugged and carried on with her conversation.

"What if it's not?" Lee asked as Gina joined her in the kitchen. "It's a dangerous job, Gee - what if he's the one in there? What if he's hurt?" She was crying now, tears that she had no real control over and couldn't really explain - all she knew was that an abject sense of terror had settled over her as soon as she'd heard the news, and it wasn't going anywhere.

"He's a well-trained police officer, Lee, he knows what he's doing. Besides, he might not even be the one in there. He does this every day - you've got to try not to panic. It's not good for you - or for the baby."

Lee knew there was logic in her words - but actioning them was another matter entirely. She could feel that her breathing was deeper than normal, and her hands seemed to shake in front of her even though it certainly wasn't cold, as she sat near to the oven that was cooking scones that at any other time would have smelt delicious, but right now just added to Lee's nausea.

"I can't just sit here, knowing he could be in danger…"

"It's all you can do." Gina used what she hoped was a soothing voice, but her words were necessarily quite blunt. Lee didn't need to be coddled; she needed some support. "You can't go and see what's going on - they won't let you near, for one, and for another you'd be putting yourself in danger and distracting James, which he certainly won't thank you for."

Lee nodded, her head drooping slightly. Gina was right - and yet all she could think of was how long it would be before she knew James was okay, before she could grab hold of him and know that he was unhurt.

"Text him. That way, if he's not involved, you'll know instantly, and if he is, you'll not be interrupting him and you'll have to wait and he can get back to you as soon as he possibly can."

The bell sounded in the cafe and Gina glanced at Lee, leant against the fridge on the kitchen floor. "Are you okay if I go and serve?"

Lee swallowed. "Yes, yes, I am. Sorry, I don't know why this has got me so worked up..."

"It's fine. I'll be back, okay? Just take deep breaths. It'll all be fine." And with those promising words, she was gone.

Lee fished her phone from the pocket on her apron and opened up her messages with slightly shaking fingers.

Heard there was a dangerous incident and that you might be involved. Please let me know ASAP that you're okay. Love Lee xxx

She waited for a response, willing her phone to beep as she held it tightly in one hand.

"Come on James. Come on. Just tell me you're okay."

But her phone did not make a sound.

Where the morning had seemed to whiz by, the rest of the afternoon dragged by at an unbelievably slow pace. Lee couldn't face going back out to the customers, so instead stayed in the kitchen, checking her phone every thirty seconds and trying not to hyperventilate. She removed Gina's perfect batch of scones and set about making her own, just to have anything to do with her hands.

"Someone's been stabbed!" she heard a shout from the cafe and had to lean against the wall to steady herself. There was a cacophony of noise in the cafe, which sounded busier than was really fair for Gina to cope with, but Lee couldn't focus on that. Instead, she entered the cafe with flour all over her hands, needing to hear the latest news almost as much as she didn't want to know.

Another young-ish girl had joined the group, and the way they were all excitedly hanging on to her every word made Lee feel a bit sick - although, she knew logically that if she hadn't been worried about James, she would probably have had some sort of sick interest too.

She didn't need to ask questions this time; the gossip was answering them all without a word of encouragement needed.

"My auntie works next door, in the charity shop - they've been made to close up, to keep the area safer," the new girl was saying. "Apparently there's an ambulance there now, and someone heard a shout - they're saying someone's been stabbed."

"The officer or the customers?" the ginger boy asked.

"No-one's sure - they still can't get in or out."

Lee put a hand over her racing heart to try to remind herself to calm down - but it wasn't that simple. Once it was clear there was no more news, she dashed back to the kitchen to check her phone once more, and then began to methodically clear, re-organise and clean every shelf. Gina was right - she couldn't rush up there, like she wanted to, so she needed to keep herself busy, to make the time pass until James would show up and everything would be okay again.

Everything had to be okay again.

CHAPTER TWELVE

At three o'clock, when Lee was supposed to be packing up ready for James to pick her up, she was elbow-deep in a bowl of soapy water, cleaning every inch of the shelving unit until it sparkled. There were no longer any stray specks of flour, nor a spilled raisin - everything was in its proper place.

With strained ears, she was sure she could hear a siren - maybe more. She didn't have any knowledge about sirens - did ambulances and police cars sound different? How could you tell? - but she was fairly sure that whichever emergency vehicle it was, it was driving away from the centre of the town.

The cafe had quietened down somewhat, although Lee knew that this would be the gossip of the town for weeks to come - whatever the outcome. She tried not to think of the possible outcomes, and instead focussed on her cleaning which was, unfortunately, rapidly coming to a close.

Upon standing, she felt a swaying sensation that caused her to grab onto the shelving unit, and she realised at that point how long it had been since she'd last had something to eat.

"Come on Lee," she said softly. "You can't fall to pieces

like this. It's not just you to think about."

As if she could read her mind, Gina appeared minutes later with a cup of tea and a plate of biscuits, to find Lee sat on the stool with her head between her knees.

"Eat these," she said, pushing the plain digestives under Lee's nose. "No arguing. You need to be eating more regularly - when my aunt was pregnant last year, she had to eat every hour or so else she threw up or had a dizzy spell."

Lee didn't argue, but instead took small nibbles of first one biscuit, then a second. She had to admit, they did make her feel better.

The bell sounded, and Lee met Gina's eye and nodded, signalling it was fine for her to go back to serving. After all, someone needed to keep it together.

She was about to take a sip of the tea Gina had left next to the sink when James walked through the archway and into the kitchen.

"I came as soon as I could - I'm sorry if you were worried, I-"

He was dressed in his uniform, and from what Lee could see it was undamaged. Beyond that, she didn't care much - he was here. She wasn't even sure how she got from the stool to being right in front of him, but the second it was possible she threw her arms round his neck and held him so tightly she wasn't sure if he could still breathe.

Then she broke down, tears falling thick and fast into the black, stiff fabric of his uniform. His arms were round her waist and she was fairly sure he was holding most of her weight, as her legs felt weak beneath her.

"Hey, hey, it's okay, it's all okay."

"I... I was so worried," she managed to choke out, taking deep breaths that made her whole body shudder but staunched the flow of embarrassing tears somewhat. She was quite glad Gina had made the decision to stay out in the cafe - she didn't need anyone else witnessing this.

Seeming to realise how shaky she was, James manoeuvred her back onto the stool and knelt beside it on the now-shining floor. He passed her a handful of tissues, which she gratefully took, and kindly looked away as she wiped her eyes and blew her nose.

"I'm sorry," she whispered finally. "I was just so scared..."

"I'm sorry. I've only just seen your message - but it was all pretty intense, and there was no way I could tell you..."

"I know. I know." She sniffed. "Were - were you in there?"

"Do you want to know?" James asked, and Lee gritted her teeth and nodded. "Yes, I was. But I'm not hurt, I promise, and I was doubly cautious today because I knew I had people relying on me." He smiled, and pressed a gentle kiss to her forehead. "Oh Lee. I'm sorry I worried you so much."

Lee took a gulp of the tea to disguise the fact that her teeth were chattering still. "When they said there was a knife - and I knew you were on duty - I just..." She searched for the right words, although they didn't leave her with much dignity. "I just fell apart. All I could think was that it was you in there, and that you could be seriously hurt... and you could've been, I was right." She felt fresh tears threatening to overwhelm her, so did the only logical thing and pressed her lips to James' in order to keep them at bay. It seemed to work; that maelstrom of emotions that had been fighting within her was channelled into the kiss, and within a moment or two both had their hands in one another's hair and had lost control of their thoughts.

As they parted, Lee found she was even able to give a half smile. "I'm sorry for being in such a state," she said.

"I'm sorry for making you worry," James answered. "And you have nothing to apologise for."

"I love you," Lee whispered, still a little scared of the power behind those three words.

"I love you too," James said with far more confidence. "And we've got an appointment to see our little baby, so we'd better not be late!"

Lee found she couldn't let go of James's hand the whole walk to the hospital. He filled her in on the less stressful details about what had happened while they walked, mainly to stop her mind coming up with all sorts of crazy scenarios. She didn't ask many questions, instead letting him do the talking and marvelling in the fact that he was here. He was okay. Nothing terrible had happened. It was not much further than the walk to the doctor's had been and luckily the weather was much nicer than it had been that morning, so the stroll together was enjoyable. Lee didn't think she would have really noticed if the heavens had opened and they had been soaked, not after the events of the morning. As they walked she sipped on a bottle of water she had grabbed as they left the café, having remembered in the nick of time that she was supposed to arrive with a full bladder.

The unimaginable events of the day had taken some of the excitement from Lee about the upcoming ultrasound, but she tried to forget what had happened and focus on what was about to happen as she sat in the green hospital chairs, a little uncomfortable as she became more aware of the water she had drunk. This was it. She was going to see her baby for the first time. Her and James's baby. The journey that had led them here had been impossible to predict and yet here they were, waiting to hear Lee's name called.

"I'm so glad you're all right," Lee whispered into James's shoulder for about the millionth time since they'd left the cafe. James said nothing but simply rested his head against hers and squeezed her hand.

Only ten minutes after the advertised appointment time, a voice called out over the intercom: "Mrs Shirley Jones." Lee shuddered a little, involuntarily, at the name. The first name she supposed she could do little about; it *was* her name after all and she would offend her mother greatly if she changed it legally. The second she was actively trying to change, but without her divorce finalised or an attempt to change it by deed poll she would be Mrs Jones for a little longer. She glanced at James as she stood up and was pleased to see the name didn't seem to upset him. For a brief second she wondered if she would ever have the name Knight. Lee Knight. She blinked a little, not knowing where that sudden dream had come from. Marriage could not be on her radar now - not when she wasn't even divorced yet. She supposed it was just the fact that she loved him and he loved her and they were having a baby together. All those things did make one think of marriage, didn't they?

◆ ◆ ◆

"Now, Mrs Jones, isn't it?" the midwife said as she entered the room.

"Please call me Lee," she insisted, not wanting to hear any more of that surname in this exciting new chapter of her life.

"Very well, and Mr-"

James interrupted. "Mr Knight. James Knight." He reached out his hand to shake hers.

"Brilliant. So, I've had a look at your dates and you look about 12 weeks, is that right?"

Lee nodded. "I think so. I've hardly been exactly regular but that sounds about right."

"Okay," said the sonographer, "Well, we'll know soon. This scan tells us what we need for dates and we can start looking see if there's anything we need to be concerned about." She paused as she saw the worried look on their faces. "I'm sure there won't be," she said, "But we do need to have a look just in case. Now, let me just confirm a few details about you, Lee. You're 30, correct?"

Lee nodded; "31 next month."

"This is your first pregnancy?" Again Lee nodded. "And how have you been feeling?"

"Sick and dizzy," Lee admitted. "I have to eat every couple of hours else I throw up."

The midwife gave her a sympathetic look. "Not uncommon I'm afraid in the first trimester but hopefully won't last much past that." She was brisk and efficient, but made Lee feel like she knew exactly what she was doing. "Right then, if you hop up onto the bed and we'll take a look. Can I have your pregnancy notes please?" Lee kept hold of James's hand as she settled onto the bed and pulled up her top to expose her slightly rounded tummy. To anyone else it probably looked exactly the same, but Lee could see the differences.

The talk about abnormalities had got her worried, even though she knew that this scan was not just a chance to see her baby. She wasn't old, she knew that, but being over 30 still surely had to have some risks. She certainly wasn't as young as she had planned to be. James, on the other hand, looked content, excited even, and she tried to channel that energy instead.

The midwife continued to fill Lee in about what they would be looking for as she put the cold jelly onto her stomach and swung the monitor round so it was easier to see.

"Right then..." She was quiet then, as she focused on moving the wand across Lee's stomach to get the right angle.

"There we are," she finally said, turning and smiling at

the couple. "There's your little one. Can you see? There's the head-" She pointed at the screen, which Lee was grateful for. "I'll just take some measurements, check those dates and see if we can update your due date for you, okay? Then you can empty your bladder – I know, everyone hates it – and wait for the blood tests."

"Yes, yes, thank you," Lee said, but she couldn't take her eyes off that image on the screen. That black and white fuzzy image that was proof, real, tangible proof that there was a life growing inside her. It took a few minutes to turn to James, so engrossed was she in that image, and when she did she realised she needn't have worried - he was just as fixated as she was. She squeezed his hand this time, and smiled.

"It all seems real now, doesn't it?" she said.

"It really does," James said, wiping the corner of his eye with the back of his hand. "It really does."

"So," the midwife said after a few more clicks. "It's all looking good, Lee, James, so nothing to worry about. I would say by the measurements you're 11 weeks. So… she double checked the calendar on her computer. "Your estimated due date will be October 20th. Now, would you like a copy of the picture?"

"Definitely," Lee said. "Could we get a couple of copies?"

"I can do you four, if you want?"

"Yes, please," James said. "I'd love to give my mum one."

Lee grinned as James brushed strands of her blonde hair from her face and tucked it behind her ear. He kissed her then, as they both glanced again at the screen with the frozen image of their baby.

James hand hovered over her stomach. "Can I?"

"Go ahead," Lee said. He laid his hand gently on the place where the jelly had only just been wiped off, feeling closer to Lee and to this baby than he had thought was possible.

The sky was turning a darker shade of blue as they exited the hospital, and Lee leant her head on James' shoulder and sighed.

"Everything okay?" James asked.

"More than okay," she answered. "I'm just absolutely shattered."

"Me too - what a day!"

"Mmhmm. Wouldn't want to repeat every part of it, that's for sure!" Lee said. They reached the end of the road and looked at each other.

"Where are we going?" Lee asked. "I didn't even ask how you got to the cafe earlier."

"I was dropped off - my car's still at the station, but it can stay there 'til tomorrow. Shall we go back to yours?"

"Sounds like a plan."

"Are you all right walking?"

"All I really want is to be in my pyjamas with a cup of tea," Lee said. "But I'll make it up the hill, I guess."

They walked past the shops that were closing up. Lights still twinkled in their windows, and tired workers were beginning to head back to their other lives. The street lamps had come on already, although it wasn't completely dark. Slowly, the nights were getting lighter and the memories of winter were fading along with the early evenings. James seemed happy to walk quietly up the hill, and at that moment Lee felt like she couldn't really spend energy on talking at the same time as walking up the steep incline.

Reaching the door felt like a bit of a mission, just like it had done that morning, but for such different reasons. Lee felt as though the energy had left every fibre of her body, and had never been so grateful to sit down than in that moment where she sank into the sofa cushions and let out a loud sigh.

"Sorry, I know I'm quiet," Lee said. "I'm just so impossibly tired…" She yawned to punctuate the sentence, proving her point.

"You are growing a human," James said with a smile.

"And don't you forget it! And I have a boyfriend who terrified the life out of me for the better half of the day."

"I know, I know, I'm sorry."

Lee leaned against his shoulder and felt her eyes instantly flutter closed.

"Lee… I'm not sure falling asleep here is a great idea!" James said.

Lee groaned.

"You know I'm right. Go get into your pyjamas, I'll make a cup of tea and some dinner. You need to eat - and then you can go to bed. When's Gina home?"

"What time is it?"

"Just gone five."

"She'll be locking up now - back by quarter to six at the latest I'd say."

"Shall I make dinner for her too then?"

"If you don't mind!" She dragged herself off the sofa and into her bedroom, which she'd forgotten was stacked with boxes in places that were meant to be out of the way. James certainly was right - there would be way more room at his place for the two of them, and the baby. They could start buying things now, she thought as she changed into her pyjamas. Now that things looked like they were going to be okay, they could buy a cot, and a pram, and all the other things that they were going to need come October. And they could tell people...

That one scared her a bit. Despite her successes in life, she had always been nervous of failure, and even though she didn't see this as a failure, there was definitely a niggling worry in her mind that some people might see it as that. Or as a mistake... she didn't want anyone thinking of her little bean as a mistake, because she knew in her heart that it wasn't. Not planned, perhaps, but definitely no mistake.

She avoided sitting on the bed, because the temptation to just sleep would have been too much and, as much as she hated to admit it, James was right - falling asleep at five without any dinner was not going to be a good way to end the day. Before heading back to James, she took one of the sonogram pictures from her handbag and studied it again, tracing the lines that she could see and smiling. She tucked it into the frame of her mirror, knowing that it would make her smile every time she caught sight of it, and went to find out what had happened to that promised cup of tea.

It didn't take long, after dinner, for Lee to doze off. She felt like this day had taken so much of her energy that she couldn't stay up to see any more of it - even though it wasn't yet eight o'clock.

She had shown Gina the scan picture and smiled as James took over, pointing out where the head was to a slightly confused, squinting Gina. James had made a bolognese that had tasted delicious, and Lee and Gina had both marvelled at where he had found the ingredients in their sparse kitchen to throw it together in such a short space of time and at no notice.

With mugs of tea, the three had sat down in the cosy living room, made more so by the candles Gina had lit and the darkness that had fallen outside. James and Lee took the sofa, and Lee had immediately grabbed a blanket and curled up with her head resting on the arm and her feet in James' lap. Gina had taken the armchair and was similarly cocooned in a blanket - it had become a bit of a ritual every evening that they were together.

"So, fill us in on your big day then, James," Gina said, hands cupped around her mug. "You're quite the talk of the town."

James' fingers were stroking backwards and forwards across Lee's ankles; she was unsure whether he was doing it consciously, but the rhythmic action was enough to send her eyes fluttering closed. As James recounted some of the day's excitement in his steady, calm voice, Lee drifted off into a peaceful sleep, knowing that she was surrounded by people she cared about in this safe, warm space.

It was about half an hour later, when Lee was dead to the world and the topic of the hostage-taking had run its course, that James said to Gina: "I don't want to wake her, she looks so peaceful there."

"Leave her for a bit," Gina advised. "You can always wake her up when you want to go to bed, and she can just move from the sofa to the bedroom."

"Are you sure I'm not in your way here?" he asked; it had been a long time since he had lived with flat mates, and he certainly didn't want to be a burden on Lee's while she slept.

"Nah, it's fine, honestly. I'm glad you're okay, after today - Lee was beside herself."

"I didn't mean to worry her," James said softly, stroking her arm gently under the blanket.

"She knows that. I think it just made it clear how important you are to her - that fear that hit her when she thought you might be in danger."

James had nothing he could say to that; he knew how important she was to him, and he hoped she felt as strongly.

"She's been hurt enough by an idiotic man," Gina said, suddenly sounding a little hostile. "So you make sure you're not the same."

"I won't be," he reassured her instantly. "I promise you that, and I've promised her that. I'm not that sort of man."

"No," Gina said, sipping her tea and regarding him over the top of it. "I don't think you are. I think the two of you are really good together, for the record."

James grinned. "Me too."

"And you're ready for a baby?" Blunt as ever, she knew Lee would have chastised her had she been awake - but she wasn't, so she pressed on anyway, knowing that she was only checking for the good of her friend.

"Ready?" James shrugged. "Is anyone ever truly ready for a baby? Especially when it wasn't planned. But I am excited, and I am fully in this - I can't promise to be the best dad in the world, but I can definitely try my best." He had a feeling he was being tested, and although he wasn't sure what the consequences of failing could be, he definitely wanted to succeed.

"Good. That's a good attitude to have to all this - she wouldn't have tried to persuade you to stay, you know, if it was all too much for you."

"I know that," James said. "But I want to stay. Believe me, it would take an awful lot more than that for me to walk away."

Gina smiled. "Glad to hear it. Just made sure you accept

your child for whatever it wants to be."

He had a feeling there was more to that comment than was apparent, but didn't push for more. "If I can be half the parent that my parents were to me, I'll be happy. They've always pushed me to achieve my dreams, but they've always supported me - and my brother and sister - in whatever would make us happy."

Gina nodded, and seemed to think through that for a few moments.

The conversation moved on to the cafe, and how different it was to run a business with someone than just working for somebody, and all the while Lee slept on, regaining the energy that had been leeched from her through the day.

CHAPTER THIRTEEN

Lee barely remembered moving from the sofa to the bed, but when she woke up the next morning - thankfully one where she didn't have to open up early - she was cocooned in the duvet and James' arms, feeling a lot more refreshed after an extremely long sleep. She didn't move for a few minutes, trying to decide what time it was. She knew she'd gone to sleep really early, so for all she knew it was still too early to get up - but she wouldn't complain at lying in bed with James for a few more hours, no matter if awake or asleep.

Slowly, she turned her head and tried to glance at the alarm clock on James' side of the bed. She was fairly sure it said seven something, so not too early, but earlier than was necessary. James, she knew, was working that day, and it made her feel a shiver of nervousness at the thought of him going out and risking his life every day. She knew it was a low risk; she knew it was something she needed to get past, but she didn't think it was going to be that easy to forget the fear from yesterday that had taken over her body.

She planned to be in for nine, to try to make up for how little use she had been yesterday - and she was going to offer Gina the following day off, since Tom would be coming in for his shift anyway and Lee was happy to open up and close to give Gina the full day.

Mentally, she began to compose the message she knew she needed to send to her mum and sister, inviting them for Easter lunch without arousing their suspicion about the reason for the invite. She wasn't sure there was a way she could do that without her mum asking a lot of questions, or making assumptions - but she thought that James had a point. Telling them together would certainly soften any disapproval.

When the call of her bladder was too loud to ignore, she slunk out of the bed without waking James and returned ten minutes later, with a mug of tea for her and a coffee for him, as well as a few slices of toast. She would like to say it was just because she wanted to bring her beloved breakfast in bed, but she also knew she needed to eat fairly immediately to keep the sickness from creeping up again.

James wasn't awake when she re-entered, and while she waited for the smell of coffee and toast to rouse him, she drafted a text to her mum and sister.

Hiya, hope you're both well! Wondered if you fancied coming down next weekend for Easter lunch - hope this isn't too late notice, would be lovely to see you both. XX

She hit send before she could stop herself, then leant back against the pillows to eat the toast, trying hard - and failing - to stop the crumbs from falling onto the sheet. She watched James sleep, feeling content in that moment.

"You're getting crumbs in the bed," James muttered, rolling over and stretching.

"Perks of being pregnant," Lee said, pointing out the coffee waiting for him on the bedside table. "Only way to keep the sickness at bay."

"Well, I guess I can't argue with that then." He sat up to sip his coffee, allowing his brain a few minutes to wake up.

"I text my mum and sister," Lee told him. "And invited them for that Easter lunch."

"That's great. I'm speaking to mum this afternoon, I'll ask her and dad to come, and then get them to pass it on to the others."

"And you're sure they'll be excited?"

James rolled over to lie close to her, toast now finished, and slowly leant in for a kiss. "One hundred percent sure."

It wasn't until lunchtime, when Lee was busily serving coffees, cakes and the odd hot chocolate, that she felt her phone vibrate in her apron pocket. She smiled at the lady at the counter, and offered to carry the plate over to the table for her so she didn't have to struggle, before checking it.

Sounds great sis, not too late for me - I'll try to grab a lift with mum! Just let me know the address. Xxx

"Lee, dear, how lovely to see you," a familiar voice made Lee drop her phone back in her pocket and glance up. The door had been propped open thanks to the sudden sunshine that had appeared that morning, so Lee had not heard the bell that usually alerted her to a new customer.

"Val!" she said, a real smile make all her features lift. "Nice to see you too. Sit down, I'll bring over your usual."

She watched as Val slowly walked to a table for two, and struggled to see how her hands shook as she tried to pull the chair out. She didn't want to offend the lady by offering to help - but she certainly didn't want her to have to struggle. Once Val was safely seated, she started making the coffee, frothing the milk carefully as she'd been taught and pouring it on to the shot of coffee to make a leaf-like pattern. She wasn't as skilled as many she'd seen on the internet, but it was certainly a passable looking coffee.

Lee glanced over at Tom, who had arrived bang on time for his first shift, and was currently being shown by Gina how to grind the coffee. Feeling like they could cope if a customer came in, she took the seat opposite Val's, feeling grateful for the chance to sit down and have a nibble on a plain biscuit.

"Hiring new blood?" Val asked, glancing around her former establishment approvingly. "Must be doing well!"

"We're doing okay," Lee said with a nod. "Enough that we need someone else so we can have a bit of time off every now and again, that's for sure!"

"And you're looking well, dear - is everything going okay for you, outside of the cafe?"

Lee grinned. "Yeah, things are great Val, thank you. Totnes is definitely good for me."

"Oh, it is for everyone. And James is okay? I heard

about that awful business up the road yesterday."

Lee shuddered. She'd made James promise that morning to keep safe, and to let her know when he finished that he was fine - but she didn't like to think of the possible dangers that could occur.

"He's fine, thanks. It was scary...but he's fine."

"Good, good, he's a nice young man that one, he deserves to be happy." She took a sip of her coffee, smacking her lips together as she put the cup back down. "Now, I'm glad you've got a minute to sit with an old woman like me, because I had a favour to ask."

"Oh yeah?"

"Yes. Now, I heard what you did for Shelley from the doctors' surgery, and I know you were a lawyer back in Bristol - a very good one, from what I hear." Lee blushed, although she had no idea where on earth Val could have got her information.

"Anyway, I'll get to the point. A friend of mine is having real trouble with her will. There's all sorts of complications with children and step-children and remarrying and what not, and although her eldest has been giving her advice... well, I'd sleep easier in my bed if a professional had taken a look, made sure she's not having the wool pulled over her eyes by anyone." She patted Lee's hand. "I know this place keeps you busy, but I wondered if you could take a look, one evening?"

Lee didn't have to think. "Of course I can. James is working Wednesday night, how about I come and take a look then, after I've finished here?"

"Wonderful. Thank you - it means a lot. She really is a dear friend, and I just get a feeling about it all sometimes... well, I'll get her to come over to mine, then you can have your dinner too, if you like?"

"Oh, I don't want to be a pain."

"Not a pain, I wouldn't have offered otherwise. Here, I'll leave my address, then I'll expect you around six on Wednesday, okay?"

As Val carefully noted her address onto Lee's order pad, she heard Gina cheer and turned her head.

"He makes an amazing latte!" Gina said, pointing at the milky coffee next to a smiling Tom and beaming. Clearly, he was a good fit for the business.

CHAPTER FOURTEEN

Once the final customer was out of the door on Wednesday, Lee locked up and speedily cleaned the cafe, knowing that, as she was opening up in the morning, she could always do a deeper clean when she got in. She found she was keen to get to Val's home and look into this will. Ever since Shelley had asked her to look into her rights in her job - something which had clearly worked out well for Shelley, who had popped in the day before to let Lee know that she had been offered a contract extending past the due date of her baby - Lee couldn't shake off the feeling that she wasn't done with her work as a lawyer. In the moments when the cafe was quiet, she found herself wondering if she had thrown her life away - not with settling down here, and not about the baby, but where her career was concerned. It had been so much hard work getting to the point where she had been - a qualified lawyer, partner by thirty, generally too busy to take on more work. And now... she loved the cafe. She loved talking to people every day, feeling physically exhausted at the end of work and falling asleep the moment her head hit the pillow, being the boss and making the decisions...

But it wasn't the same rush as she had felt when she

won a case, or when she had stayed up all night research-
ing to make sure she could counter every argument the
opposition would throw at her in court. And each taste of
dealing with the law again was making her hungry to re-
visit that aspect of her life. So, the prospect of another opportunity to use those skills that evening was enough to
make her whiz through the cleaning and be out the door
and in the car before six o'clock.

Val didn't live far from the cafe, but Lee felt too tired
to walk there and then back to her own flat later that
evening, so it seemed to make more sense to take the car.
Down a winding side street that Lee had never ventured
down before, she stopped outside the red front door as
she had been instructed and double checked the number
Val had written down.

It was a pretty little bungalow, with old fashioned
windows that were cut into quarters and ivy hanging
from baskets beneath the top floor windows. The sun was
already very low in the sky and dusk was fast approaching; Lee couldn't wait to see what Totnes would be like in
the summer - especially living such a close drive from so
many beaches.

The knocker on the door was a horseshoe, and Lee
knocked on it and waited for only a few seconds before
Val's face appeared at the door.

"Come in, come in, we're in kitchen," she said, stepping
back to let Lee pass. The walls were lined with pictures,
although the light was too low for Lee to be able to make
out who was in each image. She was ushered into a warm
kitchen, where a lady of a similar age to Val was sat at the
table. Her hair was a vivid red, which Lee presumed was

dye, and she wore a bright red lipstick that brought out the colour even more.

"Tracy, this is Lee, Lee, Tracy." Val made the introductions as she clicked down the button on the kettle.

"Thank you so much for taking the time to do this," Tracy said. "Val says I am too trusting for my own good, and when she said she had a friend who was a lawyer - well, that seemed too good an opportunity to pass up."

"No problem at all," Lee said with a smile. "I miss it, to be honest. Being a lawyer. So it's nice to have a chance to dip my toe back in it."

Val scrutinised her for a moment as she made the drinks. "You're not regretting setting up the cafe, are you?" she asked. "It was all so quick, I hope you don't feel like you made a mistake."

"Not at all!" Lee said quickly. "No, setting up the cafe has been one of the best moves I've ever made, I promise. It just doesn't change that I spent so much of my adult life as a lawyer and now I've left it all behind."

Lee took a breath; that was far more than she had planned to share. She didn't know what it was about Val, but some quality in her always seemed to make Lee speak more openly and honestly than she did to anyone else - anyone other than James, perhaps. She found an urge to tell Val about the baby, about this happiness she had found when she thought her life had been torn apart for good - but now wasn't the time. She needed to tell her mum, her sister, James' family - and then she could tell Val the good news.

"Anyway," Lee said, keen to steer the conversation in a different direction. "Let me take a look at this will…"

The two older women sat quietly drinking their tea, letting Lee digest the document. She had brought a notebook with her and, between sips of tea, she made notes of things to question - mainly clarifications on certain relationships.

It was nearly half an hour later when Lee felt ready to discuss it with Tracy, and Lee's questions generally seemed to be easy to answer - although most of them led to more note-taking.

"Are you married at the minute, Tracy?"

"No dear. I've been with Charles for ten years, but we're not married."

"Right, well that would be the first thing I'd look at then - you've not mentioned here anything about him. Sorry to be blunt - I don't know if it's because you're thinking he'll pass away first, or that it will go to him automatically. But if you pass away first he'll get nothing - including the house if it's in your name."

Tracy looked a little white, and Val rose to make them all another cup of tea.

"I'm sorry if this is upsetting," Lee said.

"No, no, I just didn't realise how vulnerable it all was, that's all. Carry on, please dear. I'm okay."

Okay. So, does your partner have any children?" Lee asked.

Tracy nodded. "Yes, my stepchildren. There's three of them."

"And three of your own children, correct?" Lee asked. Tracy nodded. "And do you want to leave anything to your stepchildren?" Lee queried.

"Yes, definitely," Tracy said. "Since the money is both Charles' and mine, we thought we would just split the money six ways after we've both gone."

Lee glanced at the document again. "That's not what it says here," she said. "The thing is, if they're not your biological children - or at least your adopted children - you need to put it in writing specifically what you want them to get. You can't just say children."

"See," Val said, "I told you it was a good idea to get it looked at. I knew it wasn't clear enough." Tracy looked a little distressed.

"I didn't realise it'd all have to be so clear. My son said he'd researched it all on the internet and I just needed to make it clear that I wanted to split it between the kids and then get it witnessed."

"And that's the other thing," Lee said. "Your witnesses can't be anyone who would benefit from the will - so not your sons, nor your partner. It needs to be someone who doesn't have an interest in it."

"That makes sense," Val said. Tracy nodded, seeming to be out of words.

"Look," Lee said, "don't panic. I can get this rewritten, it's not difficult, and get it back to you. I'm happy to witness it as well, if you like - perhaps Val and I could witness it and that way there's no issues."

Tracy's face brightened. "Are you sure? That seems like an awful lot of work. Let me at least pay you for it."

Lee shook her head. "No, it's fine, honestly, I can write wills with my eyes closed these days - it's just about being really specific, so I'll get some more notes off you now and then I'll take it home and get it written up and have it back to you by Friday. Does that sound okay?"

"Perfect," Tracy said. "Although I'd feel better giving you something for it."

"Val's offered me dinner," Lee said. "That's plenty of payment, honestly." She didn't want to take money off an old lady for something that would probably take her an hour at most. It felt good to be using her skills to help people; to make people happy; to solve problems.

CHAPTER FIFTEEN

Her mum's response to the text - '*See you then x*' - was far less inquisitive than she'd expected, but that didn't stop her from being nervous on Sunday morning when she woke up at James' house on the day of the big family meal. She'd given James' address to her mum and sister, but without any explanation - Beth knew she was dating James, but Lee's mother was currently completely oblivious. There were a few things she would be learning today.

"Stop stressing," James said as they sat in the kitchen drinking a hot drink. It was already the third time he'd said it, but it wasn't helping anything; Lee had already been sick once that morning, and she didn't know if that was because of the baby or her nerves.

"I can't help it," Lee said.

"It's going to be great. I'm going to start prepping everything in a minute, the meat's already in, they'll get here at one, we'll have a drink, break the news, have a lovely meal and then they'll leave. Simple."

Lee raised her eyebrows. "I highly doubt it will be that simple - but I'm very glad you're cooking, and not me. I'll go and get the table set while you start chopping, then I'm going to jump in the shower."

It was handy that James was used to having the whole family over for meals, as it meant he had a larger than average dining room table to accommodate them all. With his mum, dad, sister, brother and their wives, the room would already be crowded - never mind Lee, Beth and their mum.

"I was just thinking," Lee said as she collected cutlery from the kitchen. "About the last big family meal around this table - well, unless you've been having secretive family meals that I don't know about."

James laughed, methodically chopping vegetables and tossing them into the steamer. "You mean the one where you turned up at my door on Christmas day and announced in front of my family that the sex was incredible and you couldn't live without me?"

Lee blushed a deep crimson. "I don't think you're quite remembering all the details there James - and they didn't hear me! But yes, that meal. Your brother and sister-in-law announced they were pregnant then - and now everyone's meeting together and we're announcing the same thing!"

"I didn't think of that. I haven't seen Jack and Janet since January - I wonder if she's showing?"

"We never had any cousins," Lee said, grabbing the place mats from their home above microwave. "It'll be lovely to think that our baby is going to be so close in age to its cousin."

She wrapped her arms round James' waist as he chopped, leaning her head on his shoulder for a moment.

"It's going to be okay, isn't it?" she said in a muffled voice into his back.

"It most definitely is."

The shower went some way to calming Lee's nerves, but the issue of what to wear made her stress levels rise once more. Stood in just her underwear, she looked at herself in the full length mirror, running a hand over her stomach. There was definitely something visible there now - a rounded bump that could be mistaken for a few weeks of overeating, but most certainly wasn't. In fact, eating was something she was still struggling to do, with everything still making her feel quite sick, or causing her to vomit. The problem was that, while she didn't really need to hide it after today, she didn't want to just look like she'd piled on the pounds - and she didn't really want them guessing before she had a chance to tell them.

Her usual black jeans wouldn't quite do up, she knew that from a previous attempt, so they were definitely out. She'd brought a few options with her to choose from, and not for the first time thought that the sooner she moved in with James, the better. Having room in the wardrobe, and all her things in one place, would be a luxury she had been missing these past few months.

In the end, after several discarded options, she settled on a pale pink shirt dress over some leggings. It felt comfortable and she hoped was floaty enough to conceal her rounded tummy.

"Smells delicious," she said as she re-entered the kitchen to find potatoes roasting, gravy bubbling away and James chopping mint carefully for his mint sauce. "Sorry, I've not been much help."

"Do your mum and sister know that my family will be here too?" James asked. "You look great, by the way."

"Thanks. And no, they don't... I just couldn't face all the questions over the phone, but I told them to be here a bit earlier than your parents, so I'm hoping to fill them in before they all meet..."

"Ah well, my mum's good in any social situation so I'm sure it won't be awkward for long. Right," he finished making the mint sauce in a jug and passed a wooden spoon to Lee. "Can you stir the gravy for me, and then put the vegetables on in about five minutes? I'm going to jump in the shower while I've got time."

"Don't blame me if I mess it up!" Lee shouted after him

Ten minutes before they were expected, the doorbell rang and Lee was sure that it was her family. After all, she had given them a half hour head start ahead of James' family and her mother had never been late to anything in her life.

"Ready or not," Lee said, more to herself than to James, and opened up the door to find her beaming sister and her slightly confused looking mother.

"Hi mum, Beth," Lee said, leaning in to give each a hug before stepping aside so they could get through the door-way.

"Hey sis," Beth said. "Gorgeous house!"

"I didn't realise you'd moved, Shirley," her mum said, glancing round the hallway and trying to peer through the living room door. "It is a lovely house though, your sister's right."

"Well," Lee said, taking a deep breath and letting out the first piece of information before letting them into the living room. "It's not actually my place - it's my boyfriend's. But we wanted to have you - and his family - round for Easter lunch and, well, there's not a hope in hell we'd fit you into my flat so we thought here was a much better setting." Another important piece of information - and right on cue, before any shock or horror could be expressed at the fact she was dating, James appeared.

"Mum, Beth, this is James."

Lee was relieved to see that Beth wasn't thrown by the direction events were taking, and she gave James a friendly hug as soon as they were introduced. "Lovely to meet you, James, I've heard great things about you."

Tina Davis's eyebrows raised as if to say *'You've heard of this man?'* But it seemed she was too polite to say that in front of him (although Lee didn't envy Beth the drive home) and so she kept her mouth closed.

"Mrs Davis," James said, looking particularly handsome in a light pink shirt and blue chinos, the top button of the shirt undone, giving it a more casual look. "Lovely to meet you."

"I'd like to say I've heard a lot about you," Tina said, "But I'm afraid I haven't. Thank you for having us in your home for Easter." Lee squeezed her eyes together momentarily; apparently her mother *would* say it in front of him. Luckily, he didn't seem too fazed by it, smoothly transitioning to drinks in the living room.

"What can I get everyone?" Lee asked a little nervously, reeling off a list of options. "We've got tea, coffee, water, wine..." There was, Lee knew, a bottle of champagne chilling at the back of the fridge but that was for later. That was for after they had broken the news. Champagne to celebrate. Possibly champagne to mask some unhappy feelings about the situation.

"Tea for me, thanks," Beth said, looking at the photos on the mantelpiece that Lee remembered noticing her first time in this house. Lee glanced to her mother. "Just water for me for now," she said focusing her eyes on Lee and Lee alone. "Let me come and help you." If she could have she would have sighed, knowing that being alone with her mother was a recipe for interrogation. But of course she couldn't and, after asking James what he wanted to drink, she resigned herself to her fate and left for the kitchen with her mother. She was pleased as she left to hear Beth and James chatting about his police work. She knew she could rely on Beth to make the situation less tense.

"What's going on Shirley?" her mother asked as soon as they reached the kitchen and were presumably out of earshot of James. Lee's mother never liked to make a scene, although she did like to have her say.

"What do you mean?" Lee asked with an air of innocence, while in her head wondering exactly what parts her mother found questionable.

"Shirley. I'm your mother. You invited me for Sunday lunch on Easter Sunday - which, by the way, is something you've never done before - and when I turn up I'm suddenly faced with this beautiful cottage and apparently a new boyfriend who your sister knew about but whose name I had never even heard mentioned in passing."

"I'm sorry, Mum," said Lee, and it was an apology she really meant. "I didn't know how to tell you about James. I didn't want you to be disappointed or angry with me. So I just didn't mention it." She tapped nervously on the side of a mug as she waited for the kettle to boil. It seemed to be taking longer than ever before. "But it's serious between us and that's why I invited you. I want you to meet him and his family because he's really important to me Mum." Lee hoped her mother wouldn't be angry or upset when she found out a little later that this was not the only reason for her invite.

Lee was saved from any further questioning by the doorbell ringing and James' shout of "I'll get it!" Carrying a mug of tea for her and for Beth, and with her mother carrying James's coffee and her own water, mother and daughter re-entered the living room for phase two of the day.

James's mother entered the living room wearing a floaty floral dress that made Lee instantly think of springtime. Close behind was James's dad, followed by the siblings and their wives. Each hugged James, the baby of the family, before turning to Lee and expressing their delight in seeing her again. She too received many hugs and so it was a few moments before she turned to introduce them to her family. James did the honours of introducing the many members of his family, saving a grateful Lee the potential embarrassment of forgetting his siblings' wives' names.

"What a lovely day to all gather together," James's dad said as they sat down and James this time disappeared to get drinks, flanked by his brother. If Lee had had time to think, she would have wondered whether he was grilling James just as her mother had grilled her - but suddenly being the sole host in the room with two sets of families meant her brain was otherwise engaged.

"It is indeed," said James's mum, glancing over at Lee. "I've been telling that son of mine over and over that we need another family meal. Christmas was so lovely with everyone together - and meeting you of course, Lee."

Lee's mum's eyebrows almost disappeared into her hairline and Lee knew her well enough to know the question that she was screaming silently in her head: "You've been with him since Christmas?" Speedily, Lee changed subject.

"You're looking great Janet," she said, pleased that Janet's bump gave a clear talking point. "How's it all going? How far along are you now?"

It was halfway through Janet happily telling them all that the morning sickness had stopped being an issue (something Lee was silently grateful for, as it gave her hope that this would soon be over for her) and a conversation about whether Janet would be delivering at home or in the hospital that James reappeared with a tray of drinks, much to Lee's gratitude.

"Lunch will be ready in about twenty minutes," he announced. "Traditional lamb, of course mum. I hope every-one's hungry because I think I've made way too much even for all of us."

James looked at Lee and shot her a reassuring smile. She couldn't help the sick, twisting feeling in her stomach that was part nerves and, she thought, part excitement at sharing their news. They'd planned the timing together: they would announce it just before eating dinner and she knew she would feel much better once everyone knew.

A slight awkwardness gave way to chatter between the two families, as members caught up with each other and tried to get to know the strangers that they were sitting alongside.

"Shall we sit?" James suggested, hearing the timer on the oven go off in the kitchen. "Sounds like dinner's ready." Slowly, the party made their way through to the dining room and Lee made sure to position herself be-tween James and her mother. She didn't want her mum getting a chance to grill James before they'd made their announcement.

"Thank you James," James' sister said, "for having us all here today. This looks incredible." James brought the lamb in and his sister was right: it was worthy of some TV cook.

"There's more to come yet," James said, heading back into the kitchen and returning with vegetables, potatoes, gravy and, of course, his homemade mint sauce.

"Did you make all this?" Beth asked, her eyes a little wide at the impressive array of food on the table. "I mean, I know Lee didn't help." There was a polite smattering of laughter around the table and Lee blushed, but found herself smiling anyway.

"I'm afraid setting the table was about all I contributed," Lee admitted with a shrug. "This is all James."

"Now," James said, and Lee took a deep intake of breath. This was it ."Before I ask Mum and Dad to carve - because we all know they're still better at that than me - we would like to tell you something. As you all know - well, you do now -" he paused with a smile. "Lee and I have been together for a few months, and we're really happy and we hope you'll be happy too - well, excited even. Because," he took Lee's hand and gave it a squeeze, feeling the eyes of every person in the room on him. "We're going to have a baby, Lee and I."

For a moment, there was only silence, then a grin broke out across James' mother's face and she stood up to give Lee and then James a very teary hug at the same time as Beth said "Oh my god."

"Congratulations," James's dad said. "When are you due?"

"October," Lee said, feeling a little misty eyed herself. "October 20th."

Beth seemed to have got over her shock and she stood without a word and pulled Lee into a tight hug. "Congratulations," she said, and then quietly to Lee only she whispered: "I'm so pleased for you. I know how long you've wanted this."

"Thanks sis," she said. Congratulations and questions echoed around the group but the person who had still said nothing was sat next to Lee: her mother. With all the noise around, Lee felt she could turn to her Mum and say "Mum?"

Their eyes met and she saw a shocked look in her mother's eyes and something else that she couldn't quite name.

"How will it work?" her mum asked - always the practical one.

"I'm going to move in here," Lee said. "James has asked me and I just need to sort things out and then we'll live here together, before the baby's born."

"Are you getting married?" Tina asked and Lee shook her head.

"We don't need to get married, mum, to have a baby."

"It's just all so quick," Tina said. "I wasn't expecting... this."

"I know," Lee said. "I know - nor was I!" she laughed. "And now I am - expecting that is."

Their serious conversation was interrupted by James who, without Lee noticing, had disappeared to get the champagne. The cork popped to a cheer from most of the group and James began to fill every glass except for Lee's and Janet's, which only had a small measure put in for the toast.

"I'd like to raise a toast," James said, "to new beginnings and new babies."

"New beginnings and new babies!" everyone chorused and it was only seconds after the toast that Lee felt the sudden need to run from the room and throw up.

CHAPTER SIXTEEN

Lee leant her head against the cool mirror of the downstairs bathroom, and wished she had a toothbrush downstairs. She settled for swilling out her mouth with water repeatedly, and taking a few deep breaths to make sure she was feeling normal again.

"Lee?" James' voice came through the door. "You okay?"

"Yeah," Lee replied, semi-truthfully. "Just the sickness again. You go, make sure everyone starts eating, I'll be there in a minute."

"Sure?"

"Yeah, sure. Could you just make sure the gravy is not down my end of the table? I think that was what set me off."

"If you weren't pregnant, I'd be offended," James said with a laugh, and she heard him walk away from the bathroom door.

Lee took a moment to check her make up wasn't looking too bad, and that she didn't look like she'd been sick, and proceeded to head to the kitchen for a glass of ginger ale. She found it settled her stomach, at least for a little while.

She was surprised when she got there to find her mum facing the fridge. It took her a moment to realise that her shoulders were shaking a little.

"Mum?" Lee rushed over to her. "Mum, what's up? Are you crying?"

When Tina turned to face her, it was apparent that crying was exactly what she'd been doing. Tina grabbed some kitchen roll and wiped the evidence from her eyes.

"Ignore me," she said, with a slightly broken voice. "Are you okay? You ran out of there quickly."

"Had to be sick," Lee said. "It's been fairly constant, to be honest. I didn't even realise that's what it was, to start with." A tear rolled down Tina's face, and Lee became concerned. "Mum, what is it? I don't understand?"

"Am I a terrible mother?" she asked, scrutinising Lee with an intensity that made her want to look away.

"What? No, mum, of course you're not."

"Because I feel like I must be horrible."

"Why? Mum, please, I don't get what you mean."

"I love you girls, I really do, I just want what's best for you both," she said with a sniff.

"We know that, we really do," Lee insisted.

"You meet someone, fall in love with them, get pregnant - and I know nothing until months down the line? I just don't understand. Why didn't you tell me you'd met someone? Why didn't you tell me it was serious? Everyone knew Lee - everyone but me knew there was this relationship building, so none of them have been quite so blind-sided by the announcement that you're having a baby. You're pregnant! With my first grandchild! It should be all celebration and happiness, Lee, but all I can do is tear myself up over the fact that you didn't share any of it until you absolutely had to."

"Oh mum," Lee said, and now she was crying, ugly fat tears that rolled down her cheeks and were certainly ruining that make-up she had carefully checked. "It's all been so quick. I- I wasn't sure myself with it all to start with. I was worried I was making a huge mistake, jumping into something so quickly after everything went so disastrously wrong with Nathan."

"Why didn't you talk to me about it?" Tina asked, still looking confused.

"Because you're the only person who would have told me you thought I was making a mistake," Lee said honestly. "And I didn't want to think about it, or have any doubts. I wanted to jump head first in and I'm glad I did, mum - I am really happy." It was an odd thing to say with tears running down her cheeks, but it was true.

"And you thought I'd ruin that?"

"No! But I thought you'd question me, and I'd doubt myself, and I would ruin it. I needed to be sure... But I'm really sorry. I shouldn't have kept you in the dark..."

They held each other tightly for a few moments, Tina shushing Lee and rubbing her back rhythmically.

"I am pleased for you, Shirley," she said quietly as they stood there together. "I wanted you to have this clearly set out plan - but most of all, I want you to be happy."

It was at that moment that James came through the doorway, looking very confused at the sight of two crying women holding onto each other in his kitchen.

"Is... is everything okay?" he asked, looking from one Davis to another.

Lee glanced at her mum - but it was Tina who answered.

"Yes. Everything's fine, thank you James. I just wanted to congratulate Lee. Come on, lunch is going cold." With that, she swept back into the dining room, as if no-one had ever been crying in the kitchen - and, thankfully, the assembled family seemed too polite to comment on any tear-stained faces.

The drama and Lee's sickness seemed to dissipate after that and Lee was pleased about both facts. They enjoyed James' delicious roast dinner - without gravy for Lee, for it seemed that was triggering her sickness today - and all declared themselves too full for pudding for at least another hour. They retired to the living room to flop out on sofas and feel as though their stomachs weren't quite so compressed behind a tight dining room table and while Lee's mum sat with Beth, James's mum made a beeline for Lee.

"I'm so happy for you," she said, smiling. "I can see how happy you are, and how happy my James is so I'm not going to say anything about it being quick, because when you know, you know."

Lee could feel the warmth in her words. "I know it's quick," she admitted. "We both know that. But you're right - it feels right for both of us and we're both really happy."

"He's a good man, James," his mum said. "He always has been. Are you two going to be living together then? Unless you already are - perhaps my son just hasn't told me."

Lee smiled. "Don't worry, he's not keeping anything from you - we're not living together yet. When I moved to Totnes, I moved in with a flatmate and I don't want to just leave her in the lurch - but yes, James asked me to live here so we can do this together; raise this baby. He's even mentioned taking it in turns to get up in the middle of the night, which definitely sounds like a winner."

She smiled. "He definitely is," she said. "And I think that's lovely. His granny would have been very pleased to know that the two of you were here, raising a family in her house. She always loved this place best when it was full of kids and laughter and love."

On the other side of Lee. Janet - James' pregnant sister-in-law - decided to slot herself in. But Lee was quite happy to spend some time with her; she didn't know anybody else who was pregnant or who had been recently pregnant and so Janet was an invaluable resource.

"I can't believe this," she said with a grin. "Both of us having children at practically the same time!"

"I know," Lee said. "I was saying to James earlier how the last time we were all here, you and Jack announced your pregnancy, and this time we announced ours."

"I'm so excited though to have two cousins so close in

age and living fairly near to each other," Janet said.

Lee agreed: "Me too. I never had cousins; I was always jealous of these people that seem to have tons of them. It seems like a cousin relationship is a bit easier than a sibling one sometimes!"

Janet laughed. "Definitely. I never wanted to kill my cousins as much as I wanted to my siblings!" Her hand moved to cradle her stomach. "He's kicking again, always about this time he starts." She caught her husband Jack's eye across the room, and Lee didn't miss the look of contentment that passed between them.

"He?" James asked, overhearing. "Do you know it's a boy then?"

"No," Janet said, shaking her head and smiling. "We don't want to find out. I keep changing my mind about what I think it is. Today I think he's a boy. Tomorrow it'll undoubtedly be different. Do you want to feel?" she asked, and Lee nodded excitedly. It was something she never felt before - a human life inside another. She gently placed a hand where Janet directed her and almost jumped back when she felt a kick right where her hand lay.

"Oh my god!" she said. "I can't believe how strong he is!"

"I want a go, I want a go," James said, almost like a little kid, and the assembled family laughed as he too placed his hands on his sister-in-law's stomach and felt his niece or nephew kicking vigorously.

"You'll be feeling it soon yourself," James's mother said with a twinkle in her eye. "Two grandchildren in half a year eh, we're certainly going to be busy."

"I can imagine you'll be called on quite a lot," Lee's mother said. "Especially as her sister and I don't live quite so close."

"It's not that far, mum," said Lee. "You'll be seeing us and this baby all the time, I promise you." Tina Davis smiled; it seemed that was what she wanted to hear. And Lee knew that she would do everything in her power to make sure this child knew both sets of grandparents well. Her relationship with her grandparents had been one of the defining things in her childhood and she certainly wasn't going to stop her child having that strong, lasting bond if she could help it.

CHAPTER SEVENTEEN

"Well," James said as they curled up together on the sofa later that day, mounds of washing up in the kitchen forgotten for now. "I think that went alright, don't you?"

Lee nodded. "Yeah, definitely less painful than I expected."

"What was up with your mum in the kitchen?" asked James. Lee stifled a yawn.

"It's a long story," she said, "but basically she feels I've left her out of everything and if I'm honest with myself, she's got a point."

James combed his fingers through Lee's hair, taking care not to catch them on any little tangles. "Lee, it's been a tough few months - it's been a crazy few months. Don't be too hard on yourself."

His girlfriend sighed next to him; he could feel, rather than see the emotion within her. "I know, but I think I really hurt her. I'm going to try and go and see her next month, spend some time with her, show her I don't hide everything from her until last minute."

"That sounds like a good plan," James said. "And it won't be that long until Janet has her baby, then maybe we can get a bit of hands-on practice before we have our own!"

"That definitely sounds like a good plan," Lee said. "I don't know about you but my experience with babies is pretty limited!"

James laughed, and Lee could feel the movement beneath her. "I've got a couple of cousins who are younger than me but that's about it. Certainly no recent experience I'm afraid to tell you! We'll just have to figure it out together."

The next day as Lee dressed for work, she eschewed the loose-fitting and floaty tops that she'd been picking out recently and instead went for something a little tighter fitting. She knew that, at the moment, her baby bump could easily be mistaken for her just having put on a little weight but she didn't care - she didn't need to hide it anymore. She was happy and the people who needed to know knew that she and James were going to have a baby. If anyone asked now, she would be honest and tell them.

Before her mum had left the night before, she'd given her a copy of the scan and it had almost sent her usually stiff-upper-lipped mum into tears again. James's mum hadn't been able to control her emotions when she'd been given the same and had indeed cried, saying she would put it on the fridge next to the one of Janet and Jack's baby. There'd been plenty of hugs, plenty of kisses and plenty of tears but all in all she felt it was a fairly successful first big family dinner. She was fairly sure, what with James' lovely home and the nature of his family, that it would not be the last such occasion - especially since by next Christmas there would be two new babies in the family. That was a strange thought. Christmas was Lee's favourite time of the year; a magical time, a time definitely for family. She knew that for quite some time James had been hosting Christmas dinner at his house with all his family. Would they do that this year? With a two-month-old baby? Not to mention his brother's child. She found herself hoping that they would. The Davis family had never really had big family Christmases, especially since Lee's dad had left. It had generally just been the three of them: her, her mum and Beth.

Imagining a large family gathered around the table with presents and crackers and hats and children made Lee feel warm inside.

Gina was keen, once she reached the cafe, to know how the meal had gone, but there wasn't an awful lot of time to chat. What with them being closed the day before and this being a bank holiday, most people were off from work and so there was a steady stream of customers keen to get out, explore the town and catch up with family and friends - not to mention a healthy dose of holidaymakers (although, unfortunately for them, the weather had been less than clement.) Between serving, she managed to fill Gina in on most of the big events - her mother's upset, the need to vomit in the middle of dinner and the fact that everyone had, in the end, seemed quite excited.

"So," Gina said as she cleaned the coffee machine for the fifth time that day after it had once again become covered in milk and coffee grounds. "I guess you'll be moving out then." She didn't look so upset this time and Lee felt that she could be honest with her, even in the crowded cafe.

"I will be," she said, "but I wanted to talk to you about it first. I don't want to leave you in the lurch - I never wanted to, even when I thought I might be moving back to Bristol. But I hope you understand it's the right thing to do. If James and I are going to raise this child together it doesn't really make sense to do it from two separate homes. Let alone all the practicalities of having two of everything we'll need."

Gina sighed. "I know. I was being irrational the other day and I'm sorry - of course you're going to move in there and I know you wouldn't leave me high and dry. I'll be okay; after all, the money I'm making here is more regular than it ever was before and once you've had the baby, I guess I'll be taking on more hours here anyway."

Lee laughed; "I'm not even sure how you'd do that," she said. "You already work most hours under the sun! But when you're taking sole responsibility - which I guess you will be when I'm off on maternity leave - then you'll definitely be able to earn some more money. I'll make sure of it."

Gina nodded. "I was wondering if I might be able to afford to live without a flatmate. You see, I've never lived on my own. It might be nice for a change."

"Charming!" exclaimed Lee said with a laugh and Gina

gave her a gentle shove.

"Oh shut up you," she said. "You know I don't mean it like that. But I'm a grown woman in her twenties and maybe now's the time to find out what living on my own is like. You never know, I might meet someone and end up not living alone for very long - after all, apparently love comes quickly in Totnes!"

Lee giggled. "Apparently it does. Are you really okay with it then?"

Gina nodded. "I'll miss you, I won't lie - I'll really miss having you around. I've never got on with somebody I lived with so well before to be honest and - well, I know this might sound a bit funny but it was like having a sister. But you know, one that you actually get on with."

Lee laughed; "No, I know exactly what you mean. I've never been so close to a friend before - not had someone I would tell everything to. It's nice not to just stay in my own head; I'll really miss that."

"But," Gina said, "if you think I'm going to be up in the middle of the night changing dirty nappies and taking a crying baby off your hands you've got another thing coming, I'm afraid - and I would guess that James probably will do those things, so he's probably your best bet. Plus I'm sure he is amazing in bed!"

"Gina!" Lee exclaimed. "You can't just randomly say that in the middle of a packed cafe!" She glanced around to see if anyone looked like they had overhead. "But you may well be right!"

Both women dissolved into peals of laughter, causing

a few of the customers to glance around at them. Most, however, just smiled at the sight of two women having such a good time doing their job and turned back to their coffees without a word.

It was then that the door opened, the bell rang and Val stepped inside. "Val!" exclaimed Lee, the laughter infecting her mood. "Lovely to see you again, and thanks again for dinner the other night - it was fantastic."

"Not a problem at all, dear, it was the least I could do after the help you gave to me and Shelly. It made a world of difference that did, and thank you for getting it back to us so quickly."

"It's fine. I'd like to think no one was deliberately misleading her but it certainly was a very woolly will - it wouldn't have stood up to any scrutiny at all."

"Exactly what I thought," said Val. "Anyway, at least it's sorted now. Everyone knows where they stand. Did you have a nice Easter?" she asked.

"Lovely," said Lee truthfully. It was not a holiday she'd ever particularly celebrated, but having a big family meal had certainly made it more of an occasion - let alone the sharing of her news. "We had my family and James's family round at James's for Sunday lunch," she said. She knew that James's mum and Val spoke sometimes and she wondered if Val already knew the news - but she didn't show any signs of it.

"That sounds splendid," Val said. "Any special occasion, or just for Easter?" Lee didn't know if she was imagining things but she was sure that Val's eyes glanced at her growing stomach, despite the difference only being minimal at this point. She only debated her answer for half a second.

"Well," she said with a grin, "it was a special occasion actually, and now I've told them, I can tell you. James and I are having a baby."

"How exciting!" Val gave her a hug across the counter. "What amazing news! Oh, congratulations Lee, and congratulations to James too - please tell him if I don't see him. Oh I bet his mother was over the moon."

Lee smiled; "I think so, especially with his brother and sister-in-law expecting too. Two grandchildren in the space of a few months - it's crazy."

"Ah, I can picture it now. Your hair, James's eyes - that's going to be one pretty baby if you don't mind me saying! You've made my day with that news Lee, you really have. Happiness couldn't have happened to two nicer people. And if you need a babysitter you know where I am!"

"I won't forget that - in fact, you might regret saying it!"

It had probably been a couple of days that it has been sat there, rather innocently, on the table in the hallway. Lee had only been home briefly in those couple of days so she hadn't noticed it, but Gina pointed it out to her that evening as they sat at the kitchen table eating spaghetti.

"Did you notice the letter for you?" she asked. Lee shook her head with a mouthful of food and once she'd finished chewing, wandered over to the table to grab whatever it was. It was a large, brown Manila envelope, A4 in size, but as soon as she saw it she had a sneaking suspicion about what it would contain. Her address was printed on the front; at the back it was carefully sealed. She didn't really want to open it but, at the same time, she couldn't just leave it there - not now she knew it existed. Slowly she peeled back the lip of the envelope and slid out the document inside.

"What is it?" asked Gina, reaching for a piece of garlic bread.

"My divorce," said Lee with a heavy sigh. "It seems very strange to see it there in black and white on the page."

"Wow," said Gina. Lee couldn't help but think back to their wedding day and the excitement of family and friends; a little too much alcohol; promises made that were meant to last a lifetime. It was hard to shake the feeling that divorce was failure, even though she knew, she knew deep down that this was the right decision; that she could not remain married to a man who could have had so little respect for her, and for their marriage, for their vows. If anyone had failed it was Nathan, surely to God. He was the one who had given up on their marriage. He was the one who had looked for solace in another woman's bed - well, in their bed with many other women. But Lee remembered holding their marriage certificate in her hand when it had arrived a little while after the wedding, with their new address typed on front, and feeling like this was it. This was who she was now: Lee Jones, wife, lawyer, hopefully future mother. This piece of paper was a sign that all that had changed. Lee Davis: cafe owner, future mother. The last one was now a lot more secure and she needed this piece of paper to move on with her life - but that didn't make it easy seeing her marriage officially over.

"Are you okay?" Gina asked, after Lee had stood in silence for a little longer than was really comfortable.

"Yeah," said Lee. "It's just weird, but I'm okay." And she was fairly sure she meant it. It certainly didn't compare with the pain of initially finding out that her marriage was over; finding out she had been so bitterly betrayed. She hoped she would never feel that pain again in her lifetime.

CHAPTER EIGHTEEN

By the early May bank holiday, when the sun was shining more frequently and the holiday makers were visiting Totnes in more regular droves, Lee felt ready for the next big move in her life; the move to live with James.

There was a clear bump showing beneath her clothes now, and she loved it when people asked when she was due, or commented on how she was glowing. And she felt like she was glowing, as she and James took walks by the river, or sat and had dinners where they discussed the future, possible names, whether they thought they were having a boy or a girl. Like James' brother and sister-in-law, they had decided they didn't want to know; they were happy to be surprised when the time came.

They spent the last night in Lee's flat with Gina, having dinner together, laughing, Gina drinking too much wine, and when they went to bed that night both Lee and Gina had tears in their eyes. Despite the fact it had only been six months, it felt like the end of an era; a transitional period that had been so necessary for her to move on in life and make a new path.

Once the bedroom door was closed and she and James

were alone, he held her in his arms as they sat on the edge of the bed and she cried.

"I don't want you to feel like you have to do this," he said, stroking his hand up and down her back.

Lee took a deep breath. "I don't, James. I'm excited about our future together - the three of us. But I'm still sad to be leaving this flat, leaving Gina. I promise it's not because I don't want to live with you. I love you."

He rested his forehead against hers. "I love you too, my Lee."

Lee blinked her tears away and stood from the bed, standing between James' legs and lifting her arms above her head. James' eyes met Lee's and for a moment neither blinked, neither stirred, they simply soaked in the emotion that was flooding the room.

Then James' fingers took the hem of her t-shirt and gently, painfully slowly, peeled it up past the smooth, gentle roundness of her belly, past her black and pink lacy bra, over her shoulders and finally, with a last reach, over the tips of her fingers, where it caught for a second before he dropped it to the floor.

Lee closed her eyes as his fingers stroked down her arms, lingering on the waistband of her stretchy jeans. She felt, rather than saw, his lips press against her rounded stomach, trailing kisses from one side to the other. Next he slipped off her jeans, and grinned.

"Loving the matching underwear," he said.

"I like to make an effort, every now and again," she said with a smile.

"You're always beautiful," he said, and he rose to press his lips to her lips this time, letting his hands reach into her hair and only separating as she pulled his t-shirt over his head and added it to her clothes on the floor. "Effort or no effort."

"You, Lee, you're it for me," he whispered into her ear as he kissed the delicate skin beneath her ear lobe. "You, me, this child, more children - I can see this beautiful future laid out in front of us."

Lee couldn't even voice how those words made her feel, and so instead she put her love and her passion into their kisses, their touches - and as they made love it wasn't rushed, despite the passion; it was as if they had the rest of their lives in front of them to enjoy these moments.

Lee was hopeful that they would.

There were tears the next morning, too, as James loaded Lee's boxes into both of their cars. Luckily much of what she brought from Bristol was still in boxes, so packing hadn't been as big a chore as it could have been. Once the room was empty of all Lee's belongings, and she'd checked the living room, kitchen and bathroom for anything she had missed, she stood at the door to her now bare room and remembered the day she had walked in here and decided to stay in Totnes for a month or so. That decision had led to so many changes; her life now was virtually unrecognisable from what it had been a year ago.

Lee felt an arm around her waist, and turned to see

Gina. Everything had been said already, and so the two simply hugged in the doorway of the empty bedroom.

"I'm thinking of turning it into a gym," Gina said, rubbing tears from her eyes.

"When have you ever been to the gym?" Lee asked with a teary smile.

"Well, maybe I will if it's in the room next to me." She laughed. "Oh, who am I kidding - it's going to end up as extra storage, I'm sure."

"I think that's everything," James said, hanging back by the front door to give them a moment of privacy.

"Okay - I'm coming," Lee said. "Bye, flat," she whispered to her room.

"I don't know why I'm crying," Gina said, sounding almost annoyed. "I'll see you at work tomorrow."

"If Tom doesn't take all my shifts first!" She laughed. They both liked Tom, and he was the most enthusiastic maker of coffees they'd ever met. When he had found out a couple of weeks previously that Lee was pregnant, he was more than happy to take on more shifts when the time came.

"Watch him try," Gina said.

And so Lee joined James by the door, carrying only her handbag (for James had not let her carry a single box from the flat), and he took her hand in his and as they left together, sadness mingled with excitement inside Lee at the prospect of this life they were going to build together - her, James and this little baby growing inside her.

The drive to James' - well, she supposed it was both of their home now - didn't take long, with James in front and Lee driving her own car behind. She didn't have anything huge, but it would have been a very tight squeeze to fit it all into one car - and pointless, since they needed both of their cars.

As she drove up the driveway, she took a moment to remind herself that this was her home now; she wasn't just going to be a visitor anymore. There were many things that they needed to discuss, that somehow in the heat and excitement of their romance had been swept under the carpet. Finances, paying rent, bills - when Lee and Nate had bought their house, they'd bought together. When they'd rented, it had been together. Now she was moving in to a house that belonged to James, and James alone.

She knew there was no mortgage - James had told her that his gran had left it to him with the mortgage fully paid - but she certainly didn't plan to live off his money. She had her own money - and would have more of it once the divorce money came through - her half of the house, for a start. Nate had chosen to buy her out, instead of sell the house - something Lee struggled to understand, since there was no way she could have lived in a house with all those memories once the marriage was over. But then clearly her ex-husband had never had such strong emotional attachments to things, places, people — or marriages.

James was already taking boxes into the house, and Lee realised she'd been sat, day-dreaming and reminiscing instead of helping get her things into the cottage.

The sun shone onto the red door of the cottage, and Lee couldn't help watching James, lifting boxes and carrying them through the door, his muscles showing beneath the t-shirt's sleeves.

As she went to lift a box from the car and follow him in, she heard a shout from the upstairs window, and when she looked up, James was stood there, looking annoyed.

"Don't you dare!" he shouted, and although the words were muffled through the glass, she heard and understood - although she did roll her eyes whilst she smiled.

He reappeared seconds later in that red doorway, with a smile on his lips and tousled hair.

"I thought I told you," he said. "No lifting anything. That's my job. Speaking of which..."

Before she knew what was happening, James had an arm under hers and another behind her legs, and had swept her off her feet - quite literally!

"James Knight, what on earth do you think you're doing?"

"Sweeping you off your feet, Lee! Carrying you across the threshold to our home together."

Lee couldn't wipe the smile from her face. "That's for when you're married, silly, not when you're moving in together."

"Well, then I'll do it again when we get married - but this time, it's because we're moving in together."

Lee's heart skipped a beat. She didn't say a word, letting him take her over that threshold, but she knew that wasn't a phrase she was going to forget: *when we get married.*

◆ ◆ ◆

"I'm exhausted," Lee said, flopping onto the sofa. "And I didn't even do much today!"

"Well, you did keep me up half the night..." James said, and Lee blushed. "I'll make you some lunch - cheese on toast sound okay?"

"Sounds fantastic, but you did all the heavy lifting, I'll make it."

"I'm not growing a human being though. You sit, I'll make food."

"I'm not going to argue. God, it's nice not to feel sick at the thought of random foods - I hope that's the end of morning sickness now!"

They tucked in hungrily to their cheese on toast, having missed breakfast that morning, and between bites Lee said: "We should probably get everything unpacked, shouldn't we..."

"Well," James said. "We could - but we're off tomorrow too, so we could do it then. I was thinking - if you wanted to - maybe we could go and buy some things for the nursery?"

Lee grinned. "That sounds great. And maybe - could we talk while we drive there?"

"About anything in particular?"

"Money," Lee said. "How we're going to work this - living together. Financially."

"Sounds like a lawyer," James said - but he was smiling. "But yes, we can discuss it."

"James," Lee said, half an hour later when they were both in James' car and heading for Torquay, which James assured her would have the biggest baby stores in the vicinity. "I don't want you to think I'm the sort of woman who is going to expect you to pay for everything, to look after me. I know I'm not earning what I did before, but my expenses are a lot lower too - and I want to do this together."

"I don't think you're after anything, if that's what you're saying," James said. "I want to look after you, though - when you need me to. And I hope you would want to look after me, too - when I need you to."

Lee nodded. "Okay, I can be on board with that."

"And when you're pregnant, when you've just given birth, when you're nursing our baby - then I feel like that's a time when I can take care of you."

"I guess..."

"So. What are you worried about?"

"Shall I pay you rent? I presume we'll halve the bills? Will we split the cost of what we're buying today, or should I buy it? There's just so many questions..."

"You over think things."

"Comes with the profession - well, the previous profession, I guess."

"Okay. Well... I think that splitting the cost of every little thing will get complicated. I don't have massive expenses - the mortgage is paid, so it's just bills and council tax. So - this might sound crazy, and we've only been together what, five months? But we're living together, and we're having a kid together, and so in my mind - let's just put it all together. Have our wages go into the same account, pay for everything from it, make things simple."

"That's a big step, James..."

"Bigger than having a child?"

"I guess not. But..." She bit her lip, not wanting to spoil the magic of their relationship with negativity - but needing to say it. "But what if something goes wrong, James? We're not married, there's no legal protection for either of us if this doesn't work out."

"Are you planning on this not working out?" James kept his eyes on the road, which perhaps made the conversation a little easier. She thought she would melt if she were looking into those eyes...

"Of course not, James - but I wasn't planning on my marriage breaking up either. We can't predict the future."

"No, we can't," James said. "But I would never cheat on you. And if being married will make you feel safer - well, we could get married."

"James. I love you - but I don't want to marry you because it would make things easier financially - that's not a reason to get married."

James sighed. "I'm sorry. You're right - I just don't like to talk about us not working out. And I love you too."

"And - I'm not ready for marriage right now."

"But you will be, right? One day?"

"Yeah," Lee said, without having to think. "I'm sure I will be - but not just yet, with my divorce only recently finalised. There's too much to get my head round right now."

It wasn't the way she'd imagined discussing marriage with James - in a dispassionate, logical way. But, at least she felt she could be honest with him - really, truly honest.

"I would just feel better with something drawn up - some sort of agreement, should it not work out for any reason."

"Doesn't that seem rather... cold?" James asked, indicating left into the car park of the industrial park.

"As cold as suggesting marriage, whilst driving, to solve financial discussions?"

James sighed, and ran a hand through his hair. "Fair enough."

He'd parked before he spoke again, and he turned, giving her the full force of that intense gaze.

"Do you agree it would be simpler to pay for everything from one joint pot?"

"I do," Lee said. "I do. It's just the lawyer in me…"

"Okay," James said. "Okay. Get something drawn up, I'll sign whatever you put in front of me, I promise."

"Never a good idea," Lee said, leaning in for a kiss. "Signing something without reading it."

"What can I say?" James said with a shrug. "I'm blinded by love. Now, can we please table this conversation and go and spend both of our money on some baby furniture?"

Lee giggled. "Absolutely," she said.

"How do we know what we need?" James asked, looking around at the furniture, clothing, toys and other equipment that filled the shop.

"I don't know, to be honest - and we don't want to go crazy, we've still got months to go…"

"I know, I know, but it's exciting to get the room ready, isn't it?"

"You don't think… you don't think it's tempting fate, buying stuff now?"

James took her hand. "No, I don't - the scan was good, there's no reason to think things aren't going to go smoothly. You're young - yes, you are Lee - you're healthy, and I'm going to take care of both of you."

"Well, then," Lee said. "I think we need a cot, and a changing mat, and maybe we could take a look at the clothes…"

"We can definitely look at the tiny little clothes," James said with a grin.

When they got back to their home, bathed in the orangey glimmer of the setting sun, the car had a few more things than they had planned to purchase - but it made Lee's heart glow, seeing them there in the boot of the car. When he carried the packages and bags upstairs to the spare room - which was to become the baby's nursery once he or she was old enough to sleep in there - Lee was more excited to unpack them than she was about her own belongings. The smaller room that James used as an office, they had decided to make into a small spare room. It would just about fit a double bed, and since it would be used far less than the baby's room, it made sense to change them. The computer and other office equipment was to go into the corner of the living room.

"I feel like I've come in like a tornado and turned your whole cottage - your whole world - upside down," Lee said as she surveyed the chaos that the house was in thanks to her arrival - and the future arrival of their baby.

"You did," James said, pulling her close to him with his hands on her waist and leaning his forehead against hers. "You turned it upside down, blew all the cobwebs away and made it an infinitely better place."

He kissed her until she felt dizzy, and when his lips left

hers it took a few moments before she felt like she'd regained her breath enough to speak.

"So I won't apologise for the mess then?"

"Don't you dare."

"I am sorry, though," Lee said when she felt her heart rate was close to normal. "If I upset you earlier. I don't want you thinking I'm not all in with us. That I'm planning for it to end. Because believe me, I'm all in."

James' smile was infectious. "No, I'm sorry. I shouldn't have got cagey with you - you're a lawyer, you're bound to think of the legalities. And I know you've been burnt before, so you're going to be more cautious."

"But you've been burnt too," Lee said, stroking a few errant hairs from his forehead with the tips of her fingers. "By someone changing their mind. And I should have been more sensitive about that."

CHAPTER NINETEEN

While James cooked dinner downstairs, Lee unpacked the bags from the baby shopping spree, leaving the big items - like the cot and the rocking chair that Lee and James had decided would be great for middle of the night feeds - until James was there to help her. The moses basket though, that she could manage on her own. The clothes she carefully unpacked, unable to believe that in a few short months she would have a baby that was small enough to fit in those little babygrows.

"Do you think we should paint this a different colour?" James said, appearing behind her as she folded the baby grows and blankets that they'd bought.

Lee glanced around the room; there was nothing wrong with the white walls, she supposed but it would be nice to make it a little brighter.

"I think that would be lovely," she agreed. "Maybe with some stencils on the walls?"

As their dinner grew cold downstairs, they were both a little misty eyed, looking around the room that held so many of their hopes and dreams for the future.

The following day was filled with unpacking; James moved things around so she could have half of the wardrobe, and surprised her at lunch time by heading out for some bread and returning with a brand new chest of drawers just for her.

His willingness to let Lee move anything, change anything, repaint anything made Lee feel at home - but in truth, there was nothing there that she massively wanted to change.

"Have you lived here with anyone else?" Lee asked as they hung clothes side by side. She wasn't sure she wanted to know the answer - but she had a morbid curiosity that she couldn't ignore.

"You mean, like a flat mate?"

"Yeah. Or... a girlfriend?"

"No," James said immediately ,and her heart soared at this simple word. "The last woman to live here was my grandmother - I promise you that. This has been a bachelor pad since I moved in, and now it'll be a family home."

"Good," Lee said, hanging the hanger with a little more force than she planned.

"Would it have bothered you, if I had?"

"I don't know," Lee said. "But I definitely like thinking that we're making brand new memories here, together."

After a few hours, the house looked a lot closer to its

previous neat and tidy state - with a few additions that Lee had brought with her. Lee stretched out on the sofa, her head resting on James' lap as he put something on the television in the background, and she felt the efforts of the day make her ache a little.

"This pregnancy thing is hard work," she said with a yawn. "All I've done is unpack boxes and I feel ready for bed!"

James stroked her hair. "Have a nap then. We have nowhere we need to be this afternoon."

"I don't need a nap," Lee said, but she was yawning as she said it. Her eyes fluttered closed, though, and she felt James fingers stroking through her blonde hair as she drifted off into a dream world.

"Lee? Lee?" She didn't know how long it had been, but she was awoken by James' voice calling her name.

"Lee, are you okay?"

She came to with arms wrapped around her stomach, and a concerned looking James hovering above her. "You were moaning, in your sleep," he said by way of answer. "And holding your stomach. Are you feeling okay?"

She took a moment to assess the situation and wake up, and after a few seconds she realised he was right; she didn't feel okay.

"My stomach hurts..." she said, prodding it gently with her fingers as if to find the source of the pain. "It's really... cramping."

"Maybe you're hungry?" he suggested, but the worried

look did not disappear from his eyes and that made Lee feel nervous.

"Maybe," she said, sitting up slowly.

"I'll make you some lunch," James said, keen to be doing something.

"Okay. I'll just nip to the bathroom."

She felt a little dazed from the sudden awakening, especially since midday naps were something she rarely partook in. She rubbed her stomach as she walked slowly to the bathroom, hoping that food would indeed make these slightly strange pains go away. She didn't need to be worried, she convinced herself; it was just like the endless throwing up, another symptom of pregnancy.

It was once she was in the bathroom that she realised there might well be a reason to worry.

"James! James!" she shouted, hurrying out of the room much quicker than she had walked in.

"What is it?"

"I'm bleeding, James, I'm bleeding-"

"Okay, okay." He seemed to realised that she was panicking, and his voice took on a calm quality that, while it didn't sound totally authentic, did make Lee feel a little bit better - like someone was in control. "Let me turn the hob off, and we'll ring that number the midwife gave us. We'll probably just need to go to the hospital, okay? Get it checked out. I'm sure it's fine..."

Lee wished she had his confidence, but after a quick phone call confirmed that going to the hospital was the right course of action, she followed him silently out of the door and into the car. The local hospital was only a few minutes away, but Lee wondered if they would have to go to the bigger one in Torquay for something like this.

"What if something's wrong?" she whispered as James drove. "What if I've done something wrong?"

"You've done nothing wrong," he said reassuringly. "We'll be there in two minutes, don't panic Lee, please."

"What if all that unpacking was too much, what if-"

She wanted to cry, but the tears wouldn't come. Instead she stared forwards, holding onto her stomach and hoping that this wasn't going to end terribly.

She let James do the talking when they walked into the hospital, after the quickest parking Lee had ever seen.

"My girlfriend's bleeding," he said. "She's pregnant, and she has stomach pains and is bleeding."

"Okay sir," the receptionist said. Lee leant against the wall as he spoke, trying to take deep breaths and keep calm. "How many weeks pregnant is she?"

"Um, around twenty weeks?" he said, glancing at Lee for help.

"Twenty-two weeks," she said with a groan.

"And when did this start?"

"About an hour ago," James said.

"Okay. Come back into room two - I'll get a doctor to come and check you out. Can you fill in these forms, sir? And can you walk, miss?"

Lee nodded, not trusting herself to speak.

She lay down on the bed as James filled in the forms in silence, except to ask her questions that he didn't know the answers to.

"Do you have a middle name?" he asked.

"Yes," Lee said. "Hannah."

He scribbled it down on the form, and then glanced at Lee, lying on the bed. "I can't believe we're having a baby and I don't even know your full name," James said, then seemed to realise the words had come out of his mouth.

"Hopefully having a baby," was all Lee could say, and James squeezed her hand and continued with the form.

The doctor entered the room after a few minutes of a scribbling pen and occasional questions from James.

"Good afternoon," she said, reaching out for the forms in James' hand. "May I?"

James nodded, and for a few minutes she read through the information James and Lee had provided.

"Okay, Miss Davis," she said, with a gentle smile on her red lips. "I'm going to examine you, if that's okay, and then I'll do an ultrasound."

"Okay." Her voice came out quietly, and she could barely recognise that meek sound.

James held her hand through the examination, as she didn't even consider feeling embarrassed at the fact her legs were in stirrups or that there was a doctor looking where she knew blood was flowing.

"Okay, let's take a look with the ultrasound, see what's going on. Try not to panic, Miss Davis." That was easier said than done.

The excitement that had filled the room last time they had been in this position, about to see their baby and hear its heartbeat, was absent now; instead there was fear filling the room.

Lee almost didn't want to see the screen, but she couldn't take her eyes from it. Her hand in James', she felt his eyes looking to, and they waited desperately for the doctor to say something, anything - hopefully something positive.

"Okay, I'm pleased to say that there's a strong heart beat, and the baby looks the right size for a foetus of twenty-two weeks."

Lee let out a breath that she didn't realise she had been holding, and felt tears sliding from her eyes, down her cheeks.

"Now, the bleeding may simply be cervical changes. We'll need to keep an eye on you, and I would recommend keeping off your feet for the next few days, so we can make sure the bleeding stops. There is a risk of miscarriage, but at the minute the signs are that it's not going to come to that. I can't promise anything, and these things can change very quickly, so you need to come back if anything changes, or gets worse, understand?"

Lee nodded. It felt too soon to be pleased; it wasn't an emergency now, but the doctor was saying she wasn't out of the woods. She was terrified of doing something to endanger this pregnancy.

"Rest, keep an eye, but I would expect the bleeding to stop tonight, okay? If it's still happening tomorrow evening, then come back. I'm booking you in for a scan in four days, and we'll check up on everything then, all right?"

"Thank you," James said, as Lee got herself ready to leave. "Thank you for your time."

"Not a problem. I need to go and fill in some paperwork at the desk, I'll meet you out there, once you're ready."

Lee stood, feeling the twinges in her stomach and trying to override the fear that she felt throughout her body.

"Are you okay?" James asked, rubbing her back with one hand and picking up her handbag with the other.

Lee's eyes met his, and she burst into tears right there in the hospital room.

The journey home was fairly silent and Lee was thankful it was only a few minutes. She felt uncomfortable; all she wanted to do was get into bed and quite possibly have a good cry.

They got out of the car, James rushing around to open her door for her and as soon as they were inside their beautiful little cottage, James turned to Lee and said, "Do you want to go to bed?" Lee nodded warily. "Okay, I'll make you a drink and come up. Are you hungry?"

Lee shook her head this time. "Okay," said James. "I'll be up in five minutes. Shout if you need me."

When she was gone, James went to the kitchen, flipped the switch on the kettle and held onto the kitchen counter, trying to take deep breaths as his knuckles turned white from his tight grip. He needed to get himself together. He knew that he needed to calm down before he went to face Lee, but it was all a bit too much right now. Everything had been going so well, so amazingly well, but it hadn't occurred to James that something could go wrong, and now they were facing that possibility. And it was true - in that doctor's room they felt a little like strangers. There was a coldness between them that scared him and the fact that he didn't know some basic information about the woman that he was living with, having a baby with, that he loved - all that scared him too.

He knew that what he was feeling could be nothing compared to how Lee was feeling, which was why he took the few moments as the kettle boiled and the tea brewed to try to get his feelings under control, so that he could be what Lee needed: someone strong, someone she could depend on, someone who wasn't going to panic.

Upstairs, Lee had immediately got undressed and slipped on her pyjamas on. What she really wanted was to have a shower to wash off the misery and dirt of the day, to make her feel like that trip to the doctor's had never happened - but she didn't feel up to it. Instead, she slid between the covers and closed her eyes, not really ready for sleep but needing a moment to be alone with her thoughts and her overwhelming feelings about the whole situation.

She opened her eyes as James walked into the room, carrying a cup of tea and a plate of toast.

"I brought it just in case," he said and she tried to smile but found it too difficult. He sat down on the edge of the bed next to her and took hold of her hand; with the other he stroked the loose hairs on her forehead. She felt the tears sliding down her cheeks at that simple gesture and for quite a while the two sat there, not speaking but feeling a shared panic; a shared sadness that they hoped would be unfounded in the end.

"I'm going to look after you," James said. "I promise. You can stay in bed and rest and I can do everything."

"What about work? Lee said.

"Gina will sort it out for you, so don't worry about that," he said. "And as for me, I can figure something out. I haven't taken holiday in a long time; you're more important. You and this baby are more important than anything and I promise I'm going to do everything I can to help you."

"What if I did something wrong?" Lee said, voicing her fears. "What if it's all my fault? What if I'm too old or I overdid it today?"

"Lee," James said. "You heard the doctor. This is not your fault. It's probably something completely normal - and even if it isn't, your age - which, by the way, is not old - or what you've done today hasn't affected anything.

He could see and hear Lee spiralling into more and more panic. "I'm scared, James," she said. "And then in that doctor's room, what you said-"

"I was stressed," James said. "Don't worry about anything I said."

"But you were right; we don't know that much about each other." In her head she was thinking thoughts that she couldn't possibly voice out loud. Thoughts that were completely unfair on James - but thoughts she couldn't suppress. Thoughts about how Nathan would have been able to fill in that form without having to ask her any of the details; about how much she wished her mum or her sister were there; about the fact that - despite how much she loved James, and she knew that she did - sometimes you needed a history together to be able to get through things.

What if this didn't work out?

What if - and she had to fight back tears at the thought - she lost this baby? Could their relationship survive that?

She shook her head to clear herself of those thoughts. She knew she was emotional and hormonal and tired - besides, it was completely unfair to compare James to Nathan. After all, Nathan may have known her that well, but it hadn't stopped him destroying her heart.

"It's superficial," James said, "and stuff that you learn about each other over time; we just haven't had as much time as everybody else. But I want to have time with you Lee, I really, really do. I was stressed and it seemed more important than it really is but we've got all the time in the world to learn those things about each other - starting right now."

"What do you mean starting right now?" Lee asked, propping herself up slightly on the pillows to take a sip of the tea that James had brought her.

"I mean, you're stuck in bed for a few days, I'm here - let's talk about it. Let's learn all the things we want to learn about each other. I'll start - my middle name is

John."

"James John Knight?" Lee said, raising her eyebrows a little. "JJ."

He smiled truly for the first time in a few hours. "Yep," he said. "It's a family name. Can't say I'm that keen on it, but it's not the end of the world."

"At least you're not called Shirley," Lee said darkly. "At least a middle name is easier to hide. There's no getting away from the fact that really my full name is Shirley - even if I do my best to avoid it."

"I guess you could change it," James said. "If you really wanted to."

Lee replied instantly. "No, it would upset my Mum too much. As you said, it's not the end of the world."

And so for the next hour before Lee drifted into a fitful sleep, they talked. Birthdays, favourite colours, childhood memories... and once she went to sleep, even if she wasn't feeling totally sure about what the future would bring, she at least felt like she knew James a little better.

By the next day, Lee was pleased to find that the bleeding and the cramping seemed to have stopped and, although it didn't stop her panicking completely, it did make her feel better that the doctor had been right. Now she would just have to hope that by the time they had the scan in a couple of days' time, everything would still be looking good.

It was the middle of the day and James was sat on the bed with his laptop, filling in some paperwork. He'd been allowed to take a few days off, with some being holiday and some being paperwork catch-up time that he could do from home. Each had a mug of tea and Lee had a notepad and pen that she had started furiously scribbling ideas in as soon as she woke up that morning.

"What are you doing?" James asked several times, but every time he had been told that she would tell him once she was done. Finally, after they had eaten the sandwiches that James had brought upstairs, she declared she was ready to share what she had been writing.

"At last," James said but he was grinning.

"So," Lee said. "I've been thinking while I've been lying here-"

"You've not been lying here that long!" James interrupted good-naturedly.

"I know, but I'm not used to lying down for long periods of time at all, unless I'm asleep. So, an idea I've been having just won't go away and while I've been lying here I thought I would think it through properly - iron out some details."

"I'm intrigued," said James. "As the woman who turned up to a new town and decided to buy a cafe, I wasn't sure you did planning the little details."

"Oh shut up," said Lee, grinning. "I've told you that was very out of character. I am far more of a long-term planning sort of girl - anyway, you're interrupting me."

"Sorry, sorry, go on."

"I love the cafe, I do, but to be honest Gina and Tom can easily run it without me and it's making enough profit to do that."

"Okay," said James. "So what are you thinking?"

"I miss -- I miss the thrill of solving a case. I miss helping people. I miss using those skills that I worked so hard to gain."

"I can understand that," said James, and Lee was pleased to hear it.

"So what I've done here," she said, "Is I've worked out the costs of setting up business by myself. I know we're going to have a baby, so this isn't going to be for a little while, but if I work for myself I could work the hours I wanted to work - hours that you weren't working so we wouldn't even need childcare. And with my divorce settlement, if you're really sure you don't want me to give you anything towards the cost of this house-"

"I've told you," said James. "I was given it. I'm not going to take money off you towards it."

"Well then, I'll have a decent amount in savings with my half of the house and the assets - even with what I've put into the cafe, I could afford to set up by myself. And considering the free work I've done in the last few weeks, I feel like there's probably a market for it here."

James nodded. "I think you're right, and the great thing about Totnes is they look after their own, and you're one of us now - as unique as we may be." Lee and James laughed softly. "People in Totnes will prefer to come to someone who lives here, rather than going out of town. I think it's a great idea."

"You do?" Lee said. She'd been half expecting him to tell her that it was silly or a waste of money, or that she was trying to turn back time.

"I do. You are a clever woman, Lee, I know that - far cleverer than I am and I don't want you to feel like you can't fulfil your dreams because we're having this baby. Or because you chose to stay here-" he smiled, "with me. I'm really pleased you decided to, but there's no reason why you can't have everything you want. I want to give you everything you want. I want you to be happy."

Lee kissed him for those words. "I am," she said. "I am happy James. And as long as everything goes alright with this scan then I'll be perfectly happy."

When the doorbell rang the next day, James shouted: "I'll get it!" which Lee thought was a little unnecessary, considering she was pretty much confined to her bed - but she appreciated the gesture anyway. She'd had a bath earlier that morning, although it had only been luke-warm as she'd been nervous about doing anything that might start that bleeding again, and now she was sat up in bed in a fresh pair of pyjamas with her hair clean and feeling a lot more human.

Sipping tea and eating toast (courtesy of James, of course), she had started a new novel that she'd picked up from the charity shop a few weeks previously. It was a habit that had started when she'd first moved to Totnes and suddenly had lots of free time; even though since taking on the cafe she'd had far less of that free time, she still enjoyed sitting down with whatever books she'd found in the charity shop whenever she could. Now seemed like a good opportunity to catch up on her reading; she didn't want James to feel like he needed to sit by her side all day, every day. She thought he was probably going a little stir crazy too - neither of them was used to being at home without a hectic schedule.

Hearing footsteps on the stairs, Lee came to the end of her page and folded the corner, not wanting to be rude when James walked in - but her smile turn to a confused grin when not only James strolled into the room, but her sister too.

"Beth!" she exclaimed. "What are you doing here?"

"Well that's charming," said Beth with an easy smile.

"No," said Lee, "I didn't mean it like that. I'm really pleased to see you." And she was. She could feel tears welling up that she blamed on hormones, but it was just so lovely to have someone who she'd grown up with, who knew her so well, here at this undoubtedly scary time.

"I thought I'd pop down and see how you're doing," said Beth, but Lee's eyes darted straight to James. She hadn't told her mum or her sister about the scare, about the trip to the hospital - and so if someone had invited or asked Beth to come, it had to have been him. He just smiled and Lee turned her attentions back to her sister.

"It's lovely to see you, although I'm stuck in bed I'm afraid."

"I heard," said Beth, confirming Lee's suspicions. James

disappeared to make drinks and Beth settled herself on the end of the bed. "How are you doing, Lee?" she asked and Lee tried to keep hold of her emotions.

"I've got a scan tomorrow," she said. "I've just got to make it till then and then I'll know whether everything's okay." Beth reached over and squeezed it.

"It will be," she said. "I can feel it."

"Thanks Beth," said Lee, fighting back tears for real now.

"Anyway," said Beth, changing the subject. "We're well overdue a catch up. You're always so busy."

"And you're never in!" said Lee and they both laughed.

"Fair enough, although I'm afraid mine is more play and less work."

Lee laughed once more: "I wouldn't expect it other way."

"Oi!" said Beth, pretending to be offended, but both sisters knew that they could tease one another in this way without much offence being taken. "So, did I tell you I was seeing someone?" Beth asked and Lee shook her head.

"No, is that why you've been more difficult to contact than usual?"

Beth rolled her eyes, forever the little sister. "Maybe," she said. "We've been on quite a few dates."

"You're not getting serious, are you?" It had been a long time since she'd known her sister date someone for more than a month.

"I don't know, possibly," said Beth. "I'm worried that he's not my type - he's probably more yours to be honest. He's an accountant."

"What are you saying, that an accountant is my type and not yours?"

"Well, you know, he's a bit...dull."

Lee rolled her eyes that time. "Is James dull?" she asked and Beth smiled.

"Ah, you've got me there - police officer, definitely not dull, and that guy is smoking hot."

Lee laughed, secretly a little pleased by her sister's assessment.

"No seriously said he's just very stable. Got a 10-year plan, wants to settle down at some point in the future - he's very honest about it all. No game playing - it's just not what I'm used to."

"Wow, it might be good for you though, Beth," said Lee. "I'm not being funny but you are twenty-seven - there's no danger in settling down. If it's what you want, that is."

"I know," Beth said with a heavy sigh. "I just don't know if it is what I want, or if it's what I think I want, or if it's because I know it's what you would want or mum would want... I don't know."

"Are you happy?" Lee asked and Beth didn't hurry to answer.

"I think so. I'm having fun with him - Adam, that's his name - and I'm happy to see where it goes. I'm bored stiff with my job, but what's new."

"Maybe it's a different job you need," said Lee. "It's amazing how much that can change your perspective on life - believe me."

"You're not going back to law then?"

Lee finished the crust of the toast she had been eating, wondering whether to tell her sister about her plans. "Well," she said, "I do love the cafe and I don't regret my decision at all - but I am considering going back to it, working for myself, working part-time maybe. I'm certainly never going back to the hours I was doing when I was in Bristol. I had no life outside of that place and although it can't be totally blamed, the fact that neither of us had a life outside our jobs didn't give Nathan and my marriage a very good chance."

"I don't want to hear any blame about that breakup," said Beth, "that is not directed squarely at Nathan Jones's door." Lee lifted her hands in the air.

"Okay, okay, you'll hear no argument from me, I promise. I want you to be happy though Beth - think about it, maybe a change is as good as a rest, like they say - I know it was for me."

"Always such good sisterly advice," said Beth, as James re-entered carrying a fresh cup of tea for Lee and coffee for himself and Beth. It was lovely to spend a few hours talking with Beth and not mentioning the baby or the possible complications again. It went a long way to letting Lee relax about the scan the following day and she expected that was James's plan all along.

When it got to nine, Lee began to worry about her sister driving home late. After they'd eaten dinner in the bedroom on trays, she was pleased to hear that Beth was staying.

"But the spare room!" said Lee, looking at James. "It's just full of baby stuff now!"

"All sorted, don't panic. I spent this morning clearing stuff out of the office and setting up the spare bed in there. It's not much, but Beth says she's happy."

"I've slept in far worse places," said Beth. "I'd be happy with a sofa, so don't worry, honestly."

"It's all done, so whenever you want it, the room is there." They chatted a while longer but after a half an hour or so Lee's eyes were struggling to stay open. It seemed amazing how tired you could be spending three days in bed, but she felt drained and Beth made her excuses, disappearing to the little room down the corridor.

Once the door was closed, James pulled off his clothes and climbed into bed beside Lee. Lee snuggled up against him enjoying the warmth of his body in the bed that she had spent so many hours in alone. "Thank you," she whispered. "Thank you for getting Beth to come."

"What makes you think I have anything to do with it?" James asked, eyebrows raised.

"Because I haven't told anybody and she knew, and it seems like the sort of thing that you would have done to cheer me up," Lee answered. James simply smiled and they held each other as they drifted off to sleep together, trying not to think about what the next day might bring.

CHAPTER TWENTY

"We'll be back soon, promise," Lee said as they left Beth at the front door with a key, just in case she wanted to go out. Beth, who had declined coming to the scan, saying that that was a moment for James and Lee and no-one else, smiled.

"Don't worry about it, honestly. I thought I might have a quick explore while I'm here. I've always loved it round this area of Devon, ever since we came that time when we were younger - do you remember?"

Lee nodded: "Yeah. Dartmouth, wasn't it?"

"Yeah. I've wanted to come back ever since - I know, I know, I should have done considering you live here now and next time I'll come for a bit longer, but this was a bit impromptu. I've got to be back at work tomorrow, so I thought if you're going out I might just have a drive around, maybe see the sea."

"Do you need directions?" James and Beth shook her head.

"It's all right, I'm rubbish at following directions anyway. I'll use my phone, I'm sure I won't get lost. Let me know, will you, how it goes - if I'm not back by the time you are." Lee nodded. "Good luck sis," Beth whispered, giving her a quick hug and then they were off and she was off and the experiences of four days previously were about to happen all over again.

It was the same doctor when they turned up for the appointment, which Lee found quite comforting. She seemed to recognise them too. "How are we doing?" she asked and James answered, letting Lee stew in her own thoughts for a few more moments.

"Hoping for the best," said James and the doctor smiled.

"Well, I'm glad I haven't seen you here any earlier than today," she said. "I presume that means the bleeding stopped Lee?" Lee nodded.

"By that evening, I think," she said. "Certainly by the next morning."

"Good to hear. Any more pain?" she asked and Lee shook her head.

"No, and I've been on bed rest. James has been waiting on me hand and foot."

"Well I like to hear that. Let's have a look what's going on, shall we?" Lee nodded. She could feel her heart rate increasing and a tight knot forming in her stomach that wasn't pain but simply a manifestation of her nerves. Once she was lying down with her top pulled up and the jelly smeared over her bump, she turned to face the monitor and watched as the doctor searched for whatever it was she needed to see. Minutes seemed to tick by as the doctor made a few notes and the whole time James and Lee held hands and held their breath.

"So," said the doctor, and they waited for whatever it was she had to say. "I have to say Miss Davis that everything is looking fine, with a nice strong heartbeat and the size is what we'd expect. I think, although I can't say for certain, that this was probably just some normal changes and you should go on to have a healthy pregnancy.

"Ah, that's a relief!" said James, smiling. Lee felt tears sprouting from her eyes that she couldn't control but she was smiling too.

"We'll want to keep an eye on you, just in case," she said. "I'll book you in for another scan in four weeks, but obviously come back if there's anything that really bothers you, or get in touch with your midwife or your GP - but we certainly don't need to be thinking of bed rest now."

"Is there anything I shouldn't do?" Lee asked. "I really don't want to cause any problems."

The doctor smiled; "This wasn't something you did wrong, Lee. The advice to take it easy was just a precaution, not because you'd done something wrong. I'd say don't do anything you wouldn't normally during pregnancy - no crazy roller coaster rides, no horseback riding, but on the whole, carry on as usual. Avoid heavy lifting, but I'm sure you are already, and try to enjoy it - if you're stressed the whole time that's not going to help things." Lee nodded, trying to take in everything she was saying. "I know," the doctor said. "I know that's easier said than done!"

As they exited the hospital, both of them felt like a weight had been lifted. The threat of imminent danger seemed to have gone and as they kissed on the street out-side the hospital, they whispered 'I love you', not caring who was watching them.

Where are you? All good! X Lee text Beth as they left the hospital. The reply was almost instant: *In Dartmouth eating fish and chips.* Lee glanced at James in the driver's seat.

"Fancy Dartmouth?" she asked and James nodded in-stantly.

"Might as well make the most of the day off not stuck in the house, eh," he said, with a grin.

Stay there, Lee text. *We'll come and meet you.* Beth simply responded with a kiss and in no time at all they were on the front by the water, sat on a luckily empty bench overlooking the brightly coloured houses of Kingswear. James dashed off to get fish and chips for the two of them, while Lee just enjoyed being out of the house and sitting in the May sunshine.

"I can't believe how stressful this has all been," she admitted to her sister.

"I bet," said Beth. "I'm just glad that things are looking okay."

"Well, fingers crossed," said Lee. "We've still got to be careful, but she said I don't need bed rest anymore - just need to keep an eye on it, and I've been told not to stress, so that's what I'm trying to do."

Beth smiled. "You've never been great at that, Lee, have you - not stressing about things is not your strongest point!" Lee nodded; her sister certainly knew her well. James reappeared with some of the most delicious chips

Lee had ever tasted, freshly cooked from a little shop overlooking the water, and together they sat and discussed taking a trip to Kingswear one day to see those pretty multi-coloured houses up close.

"I hear Agatha Christie's estate is there as well," James said, "Although I've never been, even though I've always lived round here."

"Sacrilege," said Beth. "I love Agatha Christie. I wish I had time today but I'd better be heading off fairly soon. Work tomorrow and all that," she sighed and rolled her eyes. "I'll have to leave it till next time, hey, when I come down for a bit longer."

Lee nodded; "I'll hold you to that."

"Maybe I could bring Mum." Lee grimaced a little but then laughed.

"Yeah, I guess so. I think she's come round to the idea of me having a baby without being married."

Beth nodded. "Oh yes, I was talking to her last week and she was asking about you. I think she'd rather hear it second-hand than have to ask you direct for some reason!"

"I should ring more often, I know, just sometimes - you know how she can be."

"Don't I ever. You've been used to being the perfect child for too long. I always get asked about my life plan and why I'm not doing as well as you - well up until recently that is!"

Lee giggled. "Maybe it's your turn - maybe I deserve a

bit of grilling. She hasn't asked me why I don't follow in your footsteps yet though…"

"That's because, dear sister, I don't have a plan. I go where the wind takes me, where the feeling blows me - but then that's what you did, isn't it, and look where you've ended up!

"Oh yes, why sister you are definitely right. I should have taken advice from you a long time ago."

"It's not all living the dream, said Beth. "Believe me, I wish it was. You end up in a job you hate and not quite sure where the wind is going to blow you next - but never mind, I'm sure something will come up."

CHAPTER
TWENTY-ONE

John had texted James, and he head to the bottom of the stairs knowing Lee was busy putting clothes away upstairs while he vacuumed downstairs. "Janet's gone into labour!"

Lee hurried to the top of the stairs but took the stairs themselves carefully, very wary of not having an accident. She felt a lot clumsier now that her bump was growing so much bigger.

"So exciting!" she said. "Will they tell us once the baby's been born?"

"I'm sure they will, and hopefully we can go and visit pretty soon after - the first niece or nephew!"

"And in not that many months they'll have a cousin too." James placed the palm of his hand on her stomach and grinned.

"Two Knight babies, in the same year!"

It was the next day by the time the announcement came: John phoned his brother and Lee listened in excitedly to hear that they'd had a little boy, seven pounds exactly, with dark hair and a good set of lungs."

"Has he got a name yet?" Lee asked and James shook his head. Since Janet was being discharged that afternoon, they arranged to go over and visit just briefly that evening to their house in Exmouth which overlooked the sea. Lee had visited once before, when she and James had gone round for a family catch up over tea and had marvelled at the cute little bungalow - and especially its amazing views.

They stopped off on their way to Exmouth at the large baby shop - the same one that they had visited not that long ago to stock up on things for their own impending arrival. They enjoyed picking out a gift for the newborn baby Knight, deciding in the end on a cute baby-grow covered in lambs and clouds and a stuffed elephant which James chose.

It was a pleasant drive in the sunshine and her first sight of the sea still took Lee's breath away, even though she saw it much more regularly than she had done when she lived in Bristol.

"Can we go down after?" she asked James. "Just for a little bit?"

"Course we can," said James.

"I just want to dip my toes in the water. I love the feeling of the sand between my toes."

"Most people find that annoying, you know."

"Most people who grew up on a beach, maybe," said Lee. "For those of us who didn't have that privilege, it's still exciting. Just the vastness of the ocean, right there in front of you. The miles of sand, stretching into the distance, especially when it's not covered in holiday-makers... I don't know. There's something amazing about it."

"I know, I know," said James. "I know I was a bit spoiled growing up here. To me, though, something amazing was the bustling streets of the city; shops that stayed open past five!" "

Lee giggled. "It's a good job you've never lived in London then!" she said. "You would have been amazed every second of the day!"

James laughed. "That I would. I think I'm a Devon boy at heart - even if the locals can drive me a bit barmy sometimes." They pulled up outside John and Janet's little cottage with breath-taking views and the sound of waves crashing against the cliffs. James knocked softly, clearly mindful of waking the possibly sleeping baby and then tried the handle; finding it open he walked straight in. He found himself face to face with his sister-in-law trying to breastfeed her new son; she was sat in a reclining chair in the kitchen, staring straight out of the window at the beautiful view.

"Oh god, I'm sorry," said James, blushing bright red, not knowing where to look. He tried to back out of the door but Lee shut it behind him and Janet laughed, covering herself slightly with a muslin cloth.

"It's fine. I was just having another go at feeding the little one. I'm not sure we've 100% got the hang of it yet, but it just makes me feel calmer to sit here and look out there at all that - the beauty of the sea."

"I just said the exact same thing," said Lee, laughing a little to herself at James's embarrassment.

John entered the room at that moment. "Lee, James, lovely to see you... why are you so red in the face, James?"

"He walked in on me breastfeeding," said Janet, and if James could have done he would have gone a deeper shade of red.

"That'll teach you to knock," said John, but it was clear he was only joking. Janet did up the buttons on her pyjama top and John put on the kettle, inviting them all to sit down. The little baby slept in Janet's arms, seemingly not too bothered about them not having got the hang of feeding just yet.

"So tiny," said Lee, feeling the sight of him snuggled into his mother's chest tugging at her heartstrings.

"He's quite big, really," said Janet. "Bigger than I was expecting, anyway, considering how short I am."

"Do you want a hold of your first nephew?" John asked his brother and James nodded, although he looked a little nervous.

"I don't think I've ever held a baby this young before," he said and John laughed.

"Probably no one would have trusted you," he said, giving his brother a good-natured elbow to the ribs - before he took his son, that was. "Best get the practice in now though because it will be your turn next - and there's no saying you don't know what to do when it's your own, or so I've been told."

James took the little bundle from Janet and, other than making a few snuffling noises, he didn't seem too fussed at the change from his mother to his uncle. "Hey there, little one," he said stroking his tiny little rosy cheek with one finger. "Has he got a name yet?" he asked, and John and Janet shook their heads.

"We can't make up our minds. We had a few ideas, but none of them were definite and we don't know now whether we should stick with the whole J thing - you know, because we both have names beginning with J - or whether that's a bit corny.

"I don't know," said Lee. "I think corny can be quite nice, really. Besides, he won't know your real names for a long time - you'll just be Mum and Dad!"

"True," said Janet with a laugh.

"And how are you doing?" Lee asked her.

"Pretty well. It was fairly exhausting, and I'm not going to lie - it hurts. But you forget about it quite soon after - I'm just exhausted now, but I think that's going to be the case for a good while to come!"

"Apparently that's what we signed up for," said John, and they all laughed, knowing full well that the within the next few months all of them would be suffering from the same sleepless nights.

"And you're doing okay, Lee?" John asked, handing them both a cup of tea.

"Yeah. Tired, although nothing compared to you two, I'm sure - but all the sickness has stopped and the scan's all look great, so I'm hopeful that everything's going to be okay."

"Of course it will," said John. "Knight babies, they're pretty tough." He glanced over at his own little son and beamed. James handed the baby to Lee; she wasn't quite expecting it yet, and putting her tea down, she held onto the small bundle. He felt incredibly soft and warm in her arms and so trusting, like he would happily lie there, trusting Lee to take care of him, forever.

She put her finger on his palm and he gripped it in his sleep; she could almost feel tears welling up in her eyes at how precious this newborn little life was.

They didn't stay long, not wanting to tire the new parents and the new baby on their first day at home. Besides, they knew that John and Janet would soon be inundated with all the family trying to visit. Somehow, other than their mum and dad, James and Lee had been the first family to visit - but they were sure they would by no means be the last. With hugs and kisses goodbye for all the family, Lee and James headed down to the sea as promised.

As soon as they reached the beach, Lee removed her shoes and socks and crunched her feet into the sand, feeling each little grain as it washed over her feet.

"You're strange, you know that?!" said James with a hearty laugh.

"This is completely normal," said Lee. "Come on, I'll race you to the sea!"

"Are you sure you should be racing in your condition?" he said.

"Probably not, so you better let me win!" and he clearly did because Lee's race was nothing more than a fast walk - as in truth she was concerned about falling over and doing damage to herself or the baby - but she was still giggling when she got to the sea. "Ah, it's cold!" she gasped.

"What do you expect? It's the sea in England!"

"Come on, get your feet in it!" she said and with a laugh and a sigh he pulled off his shoes and socks and joined her, paddling in the salty, freezing ocean.

"He's gorgeous, isn't he," she said and James nodded.

"Obviously he takes after his mother not his father!"

Lee took hold of his hands with a giggle. "I can't quite believe we're going to have one of those in a few months," she said. "It doesn't quite seem real – you know, kind of like a dream."

"But it's a wonderful dream..."

"Yes. It really is." Lee looked out into the distance, watching a sailing boat on the horizon for a few moments and feeling a sense of calm washing over her. "Do you think we'll have a boy or a girl?"

"I'm not sure I mind," said James. "Maybe it will be nice to have a girl, since John's got a boy...but as long as you're fine and he or she is fine, I will be over the moon."

Lee smiled, meeting his eyes; "I suppose we better start thinking seriously about names," she said. "We don't want it to get here and have to call it baby until we can decide on something!"

And so they discussed names as they strolled back up the beach and put their shoes back on and all the way as they drove back to the cottage in Totnes. In spite of that long discussion, nothing could quite be agreed on and so the conversation was tabled for another day - a day hopefully not too far in the future, or else their baby could end up nameless for as long as their indecision lasted.

CHAPTER TWENTY-TWO

Spring melted into summer and summer into autumn almost as quickly as the tides going in and out. Lee's stomach grew increasingly larger and without any further panic-stricken drives to the hospital, she began to feel much more confident in the pregnancy.

As September drew to a close, Lee sat in the little garden at the back of the cottage, with a hand resting on the bump that suggested she could go into labour any day, not in four weeks' time glancing over some paperwork. It had been a while since she had worked in the café; she'd slowed down her shifts after the scare and then she'd become too tired to be on her feet all day. By seven months, she decided to let Gina and Tom take the reins - a task Gina was stepping up to quite fantastically. In fact, unless she rang to specifically ask about the café, her and Gina's chats were solely about their personal lives.

She did miss the place and she was looking forward to doing some shifts once she'd had the baby, once she'd recovered, but getting her teeth into law work again was becoming more of an obsession. After their chat some months earlier, Lee had decided she was going to set up her own business and had been using her time at home to start putting the wheels in motion. She had found a little office on the outskirts of the town that she could rent in order to run the business. She'd made sure her qualifications were in date and that the authorities knew where and what name she was operating under. The money from her divorce settlement had finally come through and so she could finance this dream - and even though she knew she shouldn't start seriously until after the baby was born, when she had some time to dedicate to it, she hadn't been able to resist a few cases that seemed to have just flown into her lap. She knew she needed start charging; it was all too easy to agree to things because people were struggling but she couldn't do that for everybody - otherwise she'd have no time and no money. She had been, however, looking into the possibility of doing some legal aid work - something that could give back to the people in the area that didn't have the means to represent themselves with a decent lawyer.

The latest case that had come to her through word of mouth was a custody battle - something she was unfortunately all too familiar with. She had fought many of these difficult cases in court, but she found being pregnant she was struggling with the fact that really it seemed as though the custody should go to the father. She put the papers aside and decided to leave it for the day; after all, if she couldn't be impartial, there was not much point in her doing it at all - it wasn't going to be much use to the couple in question.

Straining her ears, she was fairly sure she heard James coming through the front door and shouted "I'm in the garden!" in case he started searching for her. He appeared almost immediately, still dressed in his uniform that made Lee smile as he bent down for a kiss.

"Good afternoon, gorgeous one," he said and she giggled.

"Bloody elephant you mean." But he knew she was more than happy with the size of her bump - even if it was making her exhausted carrying it around.

"Four weeks to go," he said. "Not much longer." Lee nodded. She was excited and nervous about the birth; about the prospect of becoming a mother - but at least she didn't have to worry too much now about those worries that had plagued her in early pregnancy. If she had the baby now, the chances were it would be absolutely fine - this wasn't that early. Of course, she was hoping that she would make it to full term, and luckily all the scans seemed to suggest that she would do.

"I saw Gina," James said as he sat down in the chair next to her and closed his eyes for a second, enjoying the late September sun. September had always been his favourite month of the year: without the crazy crowds that – despite bringing the tourism Devon relied on - could make life quite difficult for the locals; and, usually in James' experience, with the best temperatures. "I popped into the cafe while I was in town and grabbed a coffee - not as good as yours, of course." He laughed.

"Of course not," she said, knowing full well that Gina could make a far better cup of coffee than she could.

"She said about popping up later this evening. I said okay, if that's alright with you?" Lee nodded with a smile.

"That sounds great. We speak on the phone quite a bit, but I haven't seen her in a while."

"She's busy with the café, I guess."

"Yeah, but it's just not the same as when you're living with somebody, is it?"

"No, I guess not," James said.

That evening they sat around the table in the kitchen, feeling like it was a bit less formal with the three of them than when using the dining room, and James cooked a delicious lasagna that both Lee and Gina praised.

"I've got to say it, Lee, you've got it made here. What a good cook!" said Gina, finishing off the last of the lasagne on her plate, but shaking her head to seconds. "No thanks, James, I honestly couldn't eat any more - but it was amazing."

"My cooking skills aren't anywhere near up to scratch," said Lee, "so it is a good job James enjoys doing most of the cooking."

"How are you getting on?" Gina asked. "It's been a while since I've seen you in person - I can't believe how big you look!"

"Thanks!" said Lee with a laugh. "But no, I'm doing well. Little one here won't let me sleep, so I've become one of those people who take naps during the day."

"Always the best sort of people," said Gina. "I was definitely one of them, before we started this café business."

"He or she seems to start kicking the second I lie down at night and carries on for most of it - where if I lie down in the day, it doesn't seem to trigger it at all. Definitely seems like he or she is going to be a night owl."

"Good job I'm used to shift work, then!" said James with a smile.

"And how about you? I'm loving the new hair - pink really suits you."

Gina shook her hair as she laughed. "I fancied a change. I'm good, café's busy but I know I've told you that already! Tom's been learning how to make scones, so that's handy. Not the same without you, of course." Lee smiled an indulgent smile. She didn't know whether Gina was telling the truth or not, but she was glad to hear it all the same.

"Of course not," she said. "But you're getting enough time off? I don't want you to be stressed because I'm not there."

"No, honestly, Tom's happy to do whatever hours I need him to - he's not got much freelance work at the minute and he can open up and cash up if I ask, although usually when we're in together I just get him to open up occasionally so I can have a bit of a lie in."

"Let me know, though," said Lee. "If you think we need to hire someone else, we can always look at the budget and see if it's possible."

"Stop stressing about me, I'm fine," said Gina. "In fact," and she blushed a little, "Tom asked me out."

"He asked you out? I did not see that one coming!" said Lee, then instantly backtracked. "No, sorry, not because of you of course - he just didn't even strike me as the type to be bold enough to ask someone as strong as you out."

"No, I didn't think he would either," said Gina. "We've been flirting for a little while but I actually wasn't expecting him to ask. I'm torn now, though - if we go out and it's horrible, working together is going to be really awkward."

"Or it could not be horrible...you get on with him well at work, don't you?"

"Yeah..."

"And he's cute!"

"Mmmhmm..."

"So I reckon you go for it," Lee said. "I reckon you're strong enough not to make it awkward if things don't carry on, but you're only going on a date, not agreeing to marry the guy. Besides, we could find someone else if things weren't really sour. If you like him I'd go for it."

"Ever the romantic," said Gina, polishing off the glass of wine that James had generously filled for her.

"Well," Lee said blushing a little and meeting James' eye for a fraction of a second. "I've got good reason to be."

"We're not planning on having godparents," said Lee over Gina's second glass of wine. "Just so you know. Neither of us is particularly religious, so it just doesn't seem to make sense to have a christening. I didn't want you to think we weren't asking you, because if we were having them you'd be top of the list. I really hope you're going to be important in this baby's life - because you help change my life into what it is now."

Gina grinned and squeezed Lee's hand. "I'm not sure I'm the godmother type anyway," she said with a laugh. "But thanks for thinking of me. It's crazy how quickly it's all coming around, isn't it?" said Gina. "It seems like five minutes ago you were saying you were pregnant and now, what, it's less than four weeks to go?"

Lee nodded. "I know, even I'm struggling to accept it – although my stomach doesn't exactly let me forget about it! I can't believe it's not that long until I'll have been here for a year, and then we'll be preparing for Christmas." Lee sighed; "Remember last Christmas, with the market and going out for drinks – oh and the snow! It seems like another lifetime ago. Who would have thought things have changed so drastically?"

Lee didn't see Gina again for another two weeks, when she decided on a whim to pop into town and go for a drink in her little café. She felt an ache when she missed the place, something she never thought she could say about a physical building, and after many days spend tidying and organising, unfolding and refolding baby clothes (nesting, her pregnancy book called it), she was feeling like she needed to see outside of the walls of their cottage. With her due date fast approaching, she thought it might well be the last time she went out on her own for a very long time, and so she relished walking slowly from the car park to the café, looking in the shop windows at the wedding dresses and the cakes and the books, before opening the door and hearing the familiar ring of the bell as she crossed the threshold into her little business.

Gina was busy cleaning the coffee machine and it seemed that Tom was not working that day. She left the rotas up to Gina; after all it was her it affected. She turned with a smile on, ready to greet the customer, but the smile turned to a more genuine one when she realised who it was.

"Lee!"

"I thought I'd get out of the house," she said. "Come for a drink, enjoy what little free time I've got left!"

"You won't be having that for a while, not after the end of the month!" said Gina. "Here, sit down, let me get you a drink."

"Decaf, please," said Lee, mindful that she needed to watch her caffeine intake. It was simple enough at home, but when out and about she had a tendency to forget to order decaf drinks as she was used to not thinking about it."

"How are the barrister plans going?" Gina asked as Lee took a seat at the counter, even though one of the tables would have been much easier with the size of her bump.

"Good. It's all pretty much sorted for when I'm ready to go back to work. I've given some legal advice while I've been here but I think I've got everything setup to actually be able to represent clients in court again - although I have to say I'm a bit nervous about going back to it."

"You'll be great," said Gina; Lee marvelled at her unfailing optimism in people's abilities. "Will you be working here still, do you think?"

Lee nodded. "I couldn't not. I miss this place, honestly - I miss the customers, I miss you, I miss steaming the milk..." They both laughed; "But probably not as much. Is that all right with you?"

"It's quite fun, being manager really," she said. "I never had so much responsibility before, although I probably shouldn't tell you that, since you're the one giving me the responsibility!"

"No," said Lee, "I know full well that you're fine with the responsibility, don't worry. That's what makes it easy not checking up on the place every day - I know it's in good hands." A twinge of pain moved across Lee's back and she went quiet for a second and rubbed it.

"You okay?"

"Yeah, I've just been having this back ache all day."

"Maybe you should sit in one of the other seats," Gina said.

"No, I'll be alright. I'll just drink my coffee and then I'll maybe get moving again. It seems a bit better when I'm walking around." It was as she took another sip of her coffee that she felt that same band of pain across her back into her stomach and she doubled up, spilling some of the coffee into the saucer.

Gina looked at her with concern in her eyes. "How long have you been having this pain?" she asked.

"Oh, I woke up with back pain this morning," said Lee. "Then it went away for a bit. But now it's getting stronger..."

"Are you sure it's not anything else?" Gina asked, and for a moment Lee started considering all the possibilities.

"You mean something is wrong? I guess... I hadn't thought..." Her words were garbled.

"Or maybe it's labour?" said Gina. "What have you got, two weeks till your due date? It would hardly be that surprising.

Lee felt like an idiot for not considering it sooner; she'd just put it down to sleeping in a weird position the night before, or the weight of her bump - after all, backache wasn't something she was unfamiliar with these days. "Maybe you're right," she said. "Oh god, what if it is? What if it's time? I'm not ready!"

"Yes, you are," said Gina, taking charge. "Of course you are. I know you've had your bag packed for three weeks. I'll ring James, is he working?" Lee nodded, aware that another band of pain was spreading through her.

"Don't panic. He'll be able to leave, I'm sure they know that this was a possibility."

"I guess we thought it might be another week or so."

"Right," said the Gina. "I'll ring, you go and sit on a chair in the back."

"I don't think I can move right now," said Lee, and Gina took a deep breath and dialled James's number. Luckily, he answered after three rings.

"Is everything all right?" he asked, presumably recognising the café's number.

"All fine," said Gina. "Don't panic, but we think Lee might be in labour. Can you come and get her?"

"I'll be right there," said James. "I'm only at the top of Fore Street. Tell her I'll be there in two minutes."

"Fantastic," said Gina, relaying the message to Lee and passing her a glass of water. The customers had started to look on in interest and Gina tried not to make a scene as Lee began to squirm, clearly in more pain.

"I should have gone to the doctors this morning," said Lee through gritted teeth. "I just didn't think..."

"Never mind," said Gina. "Torbay hospital is only twenty minutes away. You'll be fine, James will be here – look, there's a police car pulling up outside, I bet that's him."

It was. He pulled up onto the curb outside the cafe and dashed in, still in his uniform, still wearing his hat and still with the police car rather than his own. There was no time to do anything about that.

"Lee darling, are you all right?" he asked and she nodded, not wanting to speak.

Gina filled James in on the fact that she'd been in pain all morning and that now it'd got worse and he nodded solemnly before helping her out to the car, one arm around her back, to try and help her move in the least painful way possible.

"It's going to be alright Lee," he said. "Hold on, we'll be there really soon."

They sped out of Totnes on the main road and were

lucky that all the traffic lights seemed to be green. The path became windier as the progressed, with Lee focusing on the breathing that she remembered being taught to help her through the pain. Although earlier in the day she had thought this was just backache, she was more and more convinced that this must be labour. Surely nothing else could hurt like this.

As they approached Torquay, where the large hospital of the area was located, the traffic began to slow and before they knew it they were at a complete standstill.

"What's happening?" asked Lee and James shook his head, looking nervous.

"I don't know. I don't understand... it shouldn't be like this. All the holiday makers have gone, it's October! There must be something going on in Torquay..."

It was a few minutes that they sat there for, not moving, until Lee let out a groan that she couldn't suppress.

"James," she said. "This is getting worse. I'm really scared..."

"Okay, okay..." He thought for a moment then muttered under his breath 'screw it'. Before Lee knew what was really happening the blue flashing lights and siren were blaring and the traffic parted as best it could, giving them a smooth passage towards the hospital. "It is an emergency," James said, and Lee nodded; there was no doubting that she needed to get to the hospital. She had no idea how long her labour was likely to last, but everything felt fairly imminent.

"Do you want to walk?" James asked. "Or should I run

in and get a wheelchair?" He haphazardly parked the car; Lee knew she didn't want to be left on her own.

"I'll walk, if you can help me."

"Course. It's not far, come on – let's do this." He realised then that neither of them had had any opportunity to grab Lee's hospital bag; James made a mental note to text Gina about it later so that she could bring it over. Slowly, painfully slowly, they walked towards the door, with Lee stopping whenever a pain ripped through her.

At the doors of the maternity section of the hospital, James called out for help and a nurse appeared with a wheelchair which Lee gratefully sank into. Belatedly, James realised that he probably should have called ahead but there hadn't really been time for that, and it had all happened so suddenly. He supposed he had been in a bit of a panic.

They checked Lee in, double checking her name, her age, how far gone she was and whether this was her first baby, since her maternity notes were safely in her hospital bag, back at the cottage. Lee tried her best to answer their questions and ignore the rising sense of panic at the impending event.

"How long ago did the pain start?"

"Well, I don't know. I thought it was backache but that was all the way this morning and it's got steadily worse from that, so I don't really know when it started properly..."

"Okay, well let's get you back and have a look at you. It might be a false alarm, first time mothers don't usually have a quick delivery, but let's get you back and have a look."

Lee hoped she might feel more comfortable in bed; in fact the opposite was true. It was so hard to keep the pain from overtaking her mind when she couldn't walk around. She just hoped this wasn't going to last all afternoon and all night. They strapped her up to a monitor and went about checking her blood pressure. After a couple of minutes, Lee felt another pain again and saw the midwife make some notes.

"Definitely looks like labour," she said. "Let's see how many centimetres dilated you are. I'll just examine you, okay?"

Lee nodded and took hold of James's hand and whispered: "Don't leave me, James, please."

"I'm not going anywhere Lee. You're doing brilliantly. It's all going to be all right. It's all going to be all right…"

And it was.

CHAPTER TWENTY-THREE

It was 6:03pm when James sent a text to his mum and Lee's mum and then, after careful thought, to their brothers and sisters and Gina. *Baby born at 4:02 this afternoon. Lee and baby doing fantastically.6lb2oz :).* He hit send and took a deep breath, excited to go back in and see his daughter again. However, before he re-entered, his phone buzzed manically and when he opened it up he had a text from almost everyone he'd messaged asking the question that he'd obviously forgotten to answer: boy or girl? He grinned and replied - *a beautiful little girl.* Gina responded first to that one first. *Congratulations! I'll be there in 15 minutes with Lee's stuff. She doesn't have to see me, but I want to make sure she has it for the overnight stay!*

Thank you Gina, James texted back, before heading back in. He was greeted by the sight of the amazing woman who had given him this beautiful daughter, lying together in the hospital bed, looking radiant. Exhausted, but just perfect.

"She should have a Christmassy name," Lee said, stroking a dark curl off her baby's forehead.

"It's nearly Halloween, Lee!" James said in hushed

tones.

"I know, I know, but we met at Christmas time, and we got together properly on Christmas day, and I feel like she should have a Christmas name. Like... Ivy?"

James considered it for a moment. "Or Holly?"

"Holly... Holly. I like it. Definitely a Christmas name, and nothing crazily old fashioned like mine or my sister's." She kissed the sleeping baby on the forehead.

"Hello, Holly."

"Holly... Davis?" James asked, his voice a little louder than a whisper. It was a question that somehow had not come up - and yet here they were, with a baby with a first name but a choice of two surnames.

"Holly Knight," Lee said, after a moment or two of silence. "I think Holly Knight. It's a shame, that I don't have the same surname as her, but I think-"

"What if you did?" James asked, and it took Lee's sleep-deprived brain a few seconds to catch up. "What if all three of us were Knights?"

"James, I-" She didn't know what she planned to say, only that her head was too muddled for anything less than a direct question - but she was interrupted by James kneeling on the hospital floor next to the white hospital bed where she lay.

"Lee Davis - you are the love of my life. I never thought I would be so lucky as to meet someone as fantastic, as clever, as funny as you are - and now you've made my life complete with the most precious daughter. Lee - will you marry me?"

And there was a ring, and there were tears from both parties - although, thankfully not from Holly just yet. What Lee had taken to be a spur of the moment decision had clearly been planned some time in advance; the ring was evidence of that.

Marriage had been something Lee had aspired to when she was dating Nathan. Marriage had been something that had defined her, and something that had nearly destroyed her. Nearly a year ago, she had considered swearing off marriage forever; denouncing it as something that could never succeed. And yet now... Now, when she looked into the eyes of a man who loved her, a man who she truly believed would always be there for her and for their daughter no matter what, the idea of that commitment didn't seem so terrifying anymore. She would do things differently this time.

"I need us to make a promise, first," she said, wiping tears from her eyes that she hadn't even realised had started.

"Anything," James insisted. Lee smiled.

"I want us both to promise that we will always make time for each other. Every day, no matter what else is going on in our lives, we will find some time for one another. I don't want to make the same mistakes again."

"I promise, Lee. I swear to you I won't let my job take over - I'll find time every single day for you, and for Holly."

"I promise too. And yes, James. Yes, I will marry you."

EPILOGUE

"Come on, nearly there," Lee said, feeling a touch out of breath herself. The climb had been steep, and even though she was used to chasing a three-year-old around, she could still use a little more cardio exercise to get into shape. James was lagging behind, but Lee knew full well that was because Holly was dawdling, and there wasn't much in the world that James wouldn't give in to when it came to his daughter. So the two of them were a little way behind Lee, despite the fact that she knew James' job kept her far fitter than she was.

"Coming mummy!" Holly answered, speeding up a little with her short little steps. Her blond hair felt in wisps around her face and the purple headband kept it from flying in her face - which it regularly did. James laughed and swept Holly off her feet, carrying her with one arm around her waist as if it was no effort at all - even though Lee knew from experience that Holly was not that easy to lift these days.

"Come on monster, we can beat mummy!" Lee laughed as James strode up the hill, giggling daughter under one arm, easily overtaking Lee and plumping Holly down on the ground at the foot of the castle.

"We won, we won, we won!" Holly repeated, running

round in circles before flopping on the floor, her puppy-like burst of energy gone - for the moment.

"We made it," Lee said, taking one of her daughter's hands as James took the other. "One... two... three... wheeee!" They swung her forwards, delighting in her shrieks and giggles, and forgetting as they always did that this game always ended with her demanding 'more!' over and over again.

"Let's see the view," James said, distracting her for a little while. Before Lee could protest, he swung Holly up so she could stand on the ancient wall of the castle, and look down at the town sprawled beneath them. At least his arm was tightly around her waist, she told herself - although it didn't stop her keeping hold of the little girl's hand too, just in case.

"Wow." They family of three stood in silence for a few minutes, looking out over the sun-kissed town that they called home. This little walk had been James' idea; he'd been up there several times as a kid, but it was somewhere he'd never taken Lee until now. The vantage point made the town look almost like a toy - little buildings, people, trees, so tiny that you could imagine they could be picked up and moved wherever you liked.

"There's mummy's cafe," James said, pointing out roughly where it would be at the bottom of the high street. "And there's daddy's police car!"

"That's not yours!" Lee said with a laugh. "Yours is at the station."

"Oh, okay, a car *like* daddy's police car. And our home is up there, behind those trees."

"Where does Aunty Beth live?" Holly asked, and she followed the direction of James' pointing finger carefully with her eyes. Beth had certainly become a firm favourite with her only niece.

"Name three things you love about living here," Lee said, shielding her eyes from the sun as she looked at her husband. "Go."

"The people," he said, without a thought. "The land-scapes... And the laid back attitudes." He grinned, lifting Holly carefully down from the wall, before placing a kiss on Lee's lips. "But first and foremost, it's got to be the people living here."

"Agreed," Lee said. "It's what made me fall in love with Totnes in the first place!"

Thank you for reading 'Lawyers and Lattes'! Rejoin Lee, James, Holly and Lee's sister Beth in Book Three: Feeling the Fireworks (http://mybook.to/feelingthefireworks). Read on for a sneak peak!

FEELING THE FIREWORKS

CHAPTER ONE

It was the same old routine, the same old commute, the same luke-warm coffee that Elizabeth Davis had every morning. She tried not to contemplate how little had changed in her life over the last few years, but sometimes - like today, when she was stuck in traffic trying to get into the centre of Exeter, having left a little too late (as usual) - it was hard to not let her mind wander.

She had once thought she was the daredevil of the family: the one who would stay up all night drinking at a moment's notice; the one who went through jobs and men at a rate of knots; the one who didn't feel the need to have her life mapped out in front of her.

And then she found herself stuck in a rut. Keeping the same job, because even though it was going nowhere, she had rent and bills to pay - and was sick of having to run to her mum or her sister for a bailout. Feeling too tired for those all night drinking sessions, because the early starts took their toll. Well, that and the fact that, at twenty-eight, most of her friends were no longer in the let's-do-tequila-shots-till-4am phase of their lives. No, they had steady boyfriends (something Beth had little experience of), or husbands, or children, or even *mortgages.*

"Get over onto your side!" she screamed at a lorry that had swerved far too close to her lane for comfort - but the distraction did at least stop her mulling over her life - for a few moments, at least. She waved at the security guard as she parked in the little car park that was attached to the printing firm she'd been at for the last two years. She always wondered why on earth they needed a security guard - nothing exciting ever happened at Chilster and co.

She'd started on an internship, even though she'd been way too old to be an intern, really, when she'd thought she might be interested in a career in publishing. That had fizzled out by the second month, but she - and they - had realised that she made a pretty good secretary, and so when a maternity role had come up, she'd been the obvious candidate. Then when it became permanent... well, it paid the bills. It definitely was not her passion; it definitely was not a career that she thought she would be pursuing for the rest of her life - but Beth had long ago come to the conclusion that she was not one for life plans and long term goals.

Her sister, on the other hand, always had been. Beth supposed that was what always made her feel like a rebel - her older sister Shirley (who was not quite as old as the name suggested, and went by Lee) had *always* been the good one. She'd gone to university, got a career in law, got married, bought a house, got made a partner by the time she was thirty... everything their mother, with her habit of naming her daughters as if they were already in their seventies, had ever wanted.

And then...

And then Lee's seemingly perfect life had been ripped to shreds by her cheating husband, and before Beth knew it, she was no longer the rebel of the family. Oh no, Lee left her home, her job, moved to the middle of nowhere in Devon, bought a café... the list of shocking events was endless. Then there was the fact that Lee had met a drop dead gorgeous police officer, had a child with him and was currently engaged!

It had certainly been a whirlwind year in the Davis family - and it put Beth's life rather into perspective.

"Morning Beth!" called Jasmine, the latest intern. At 23, she was a few years younger than Beth, but Beth found they had a lot in common - certainly more than she did with the thirty- and forty-year-old publishers that she generally worked with.

"Lunch out today?" Beth called over, dumping her bag on her desk and accidentally knocking a few errant paperclips off the table as she did so.

Jasmine gave her a thumbs up, and Beth smiled to herself at the glare they both got from Victoria, the ancient (or at least she seemed it to Beth) head of accounts. Jasmine and Beth's high energy never seemed to go down that well at work... but then, to be fair, the energy was quite often directed away from their actual workloads, and towards things like where and when to have lunch, or whether they could make it to the shops to look round the sales before they closed.

The smile dropped off her face fairly rapidly as she turned on her computer and was faced with a surprisingly full inbox. The mundane task of wading through and clearing emails - some of which were trying to get her buy something, some of which were authors trying to get their work seen, some of which were just spam - signalled the start of yet another morning in a job which, she had to admit, wasn't going anywhere.

❖ ❖ ❖

Lunch with Jasmine was, as usual, the highlight of her day. They had discussed the guy Jasmine was currently seeing - an IT technician from two doors up - and how he wanted to introduce her to his mother.

"I don't do meeting the parents," Jasmine said, rolling her eyes and tossing her raven-black hair across one shoulder dramatically. "Never have done."

"You're only twenty-three!" Beth reminded her with a laugh. "But I get you, I've never been the meet-the-parents type either."

"Besides, I'm hardly going to introduce him to my parents. They'll freak out if they find out I'm dating someone who's not Indian, you know what they're like-" Beth had never met them, but Jasmine had complained about them and their puritanical views enough that she felt as though she did. "I'm not crossing that bridge unless it's someone I'm going to spend the rest of my life with."

"And I take it you don't think Joe is?"

"No..." she said, gazing off into the distance as she often did. "No, I don't think he is. He's great for now, though..." she said, with a dirty laugh that had Beth laughing along with her.

"And what about you?" Jasmine asked, turning her eyes back on Beth. "How's things with what's-his-name?"

"Dean? Over before it started, if I'm honest..."

"What happened?"

"Nothing major, no big drama to report, I'm afraid! He asked me out, we went to a nice bar, saw him again for dinner last Thursday, he asked me back to his…"

Jasmine wiggled her eyebrows suggestively and Beth giggled.

"But the spark just wasn't there…"

"You don't need fireworks with every guy!" Jasmine said, sipping her coffee as she checked her watch. Five minutes 'til they needed to head back to the office.

"I'm not wasting time and energy on somebody with no fireworks, Jas - too old for that nonsense!"

"Pfft, not that old!"

"Not that far off thirty, I'm afraid to say - and my sister's nearly married again with a kid!"

"Do you want a kid, now, really?"

"Well, no, obviously…"

"Stop whining then and live life while you're young, free and single. Let's go out, Saturday night - you and me. I bet we can find you some fireworks…"

◆ ◆ ◆

By six, Beth was home in her little flat, with its mismatched pillows and throws and last night's plate (and wine glass!) still sitting on the side. It was quiet, as it always was, and she dumped her bag and coat, as well as a bag of food shopping she'd picked up on her way home, onto the kitchen counter. Lunch with Jasmine always lifted her spirits, but coming home to a silent, empty flat and dinner for one brought them right back down again.

Luckily, her phone rang before she could get too down in the doldrums again, and a smile lit up her face as she saw her sister's name on the screen.

"Shirley!" she answered with a grin, as her sister threw some abuse down the line for using her given name. "I hope my favourite niece can't hear those terrible words you're calling her aunty!"

"Well don't call me Shirley then, *Elizabeth*," Lee retorted.

"How are you sis?"

"All good here," Lee said. "Exhausted, Holly seems to have stopped sleeping through the night again... apparently not that uncommon at 8 months, but just when I thought we were getting somewhere..."

"Is James doing his fair share?"

She could hear her sister smiling through the phone. "Yeah, he's up at least as much as I am, even though he's the one working full time..." Lee's fiancé and the father of her baby, James, was a police officer in rural Devon - and Beth was fairly sure the uniform had been one of the things that first caught Lee's eye.

"How's the café?"

"It's doing great actually - I've started doing a day a week, just to get myself back into it, but what with the law work I'm taking on too, I have to admit I'm not in there as much as I like. Gina runs it amazingly though, so I don't need to worry!"

"Don't work yourself too hard - you don't want to burn out!"

"I'm good Beth, promise. And how's things with you? How's the job?"

"Eh," Beth said, unable to hide her apathy. "It's a job. Pays the bills..."

"Have you got any holiday due?" Lee asked. "You know we'd love to see you - the weather's nice, we could go to the beach, take Holly - and June's the best time really, before the kids break up from school and the grockles invade for the season."

"Grockles?!" Beth asked with a laugh.

"Sorry, sorry, the Devon lingo gets to you in the end. Tourists!"

"Well I'll be one of those tourists, won't I! But that does sound great... let me check with work, and get back to you, okay?"

"You're always welcome Beth - say the word, the spare room's yours."

Beth felt a flash of guilt - she really ought to visit her sister more, she knew. Whenever they did spend time together it was so great - but they were both busy, and it was easy for weeks or even months to pass by without meeting in person.

"I promise, I'll come down soon - the beaches are calling to me!"

Available to buy on Amazon today! Mybook.to/ feelingthefireworks

AFTERWORD

Thank you so much for reading *Lawyers and Lattes*! After writing 'The Worst Christmas Ever?' – available on Amazon (mybook.to/worstchristmas) – I felt that Lee and James' story was not over, and so I hope you enjoyed following them through as they create their own happily-ever-after in the South West of England.

Devon, and the South Hams in particular, also has a special place in my heart. I was born and grew up in the South Hams, visiting Totnes and Dartmouth regularly. As a student at university, Totnes was where I took the train to when I came home, and it's still somewhere I visit every time I visit my parents. It has a special something to it that I've not come across anywhere else.

I hope you enjoyed *Lawyers and Lattes* - rest assured, this won't be the last you'll hear of Lee, James, Holly or Lee's sister Beth – or the beautiful South Hams. I'd love to hear your thoughts on Lee's story – email rebeccapaulinyi@gmail.com and I'll be happy to reply! You can sign up for my newsletter here (tiny.cc/paulinyi) to get news of new novels, free stories and the occasional cute pictures of my daughter and dog!

BOOKS IN THIS SERIES

The South West Series

Love, laughter and new beginnings in rural South West England.

The Worst Christmas Ever?

Can the magic of the Christmas season be rediscovered in a small Devon town?

When Shirley 'Lee' Jones returns home from an awful day at the office, the last thing she expects to find is her husband in bed with another woman. Six weeks until Christmas, and Lee finds the life she had so carefully planned has been utterly decimated.

Hurt, angry and confused, Lee makes a whirlwind decision to drive her problems away and ends up in Totnes, an eccentric town in the heart of Devon. As Christmas approaches, Lee tries to figure out what path her life will follow now, as she looks at it from the perspective of a soon-to-be 31-year-old divorcée.

Can she ever return to her normal life? Or is a new reality - and a new man - on the horizon?

Finding herself and flirting with the handsome local police officer might just make this the best Christmas ever.

Lawyers And Lattes

A new home, a new man, and a new career are all great - but do they always lead to happily-ever-after?

Shirley 'Lee' Jones has made some spontaneous and sometimes questionable decisions since the breakup of her marriage, but deciding to remain in the quirky town of Totnes has got to be the biggest decision so far. Now Lee has a new business, gorgeous man, and friends keeping life interesting. But when questions of law crop up in her life again, she finds herself yearning for the career and the life plan she gave up when she left everything behind.

And when unexpected news tests her relationship, her resolve, and everything tying her to her life, Lee must decide between the person she is and the person she wants to become.

Sometimes decisions about life, law, and love all reside in grey areas. Will Lee's newfound happiness in Devon be short-lived? Or could her new life give her the chance to have everything she's ever wanted?

Feeling The Fireworks

Can Beth rekindle her passion for life and love in picturesque Dartmouth?

When Beth Davis made a whirlwind decision to move to picturesque Dartmouth to shake up her repetitive life, the last thing she expected to find was a passion in life - or a man who could make her feel fireworks.

A change in home and job seems like exactly what Beth needs to blow away the cobwebs that have been forming around her dead-end job. With little money to her name and no real plan, Beth needs to make things work, fast - without relying on her big sister Lee to bail her out.

When she meets the handsome, mysterious Caspian in a daring late-night swim, she instantly feels fireworks that she had long forgotten. Can Dartmouth - and Caspian - re-awaken her passion for life and love?

'Feeling the Fireworks' is Book 3 in the South West Series but can be read as a standalone novel. Fall in love with Devon today!

The Best Christmas Ever

A Devon wedding with the magic of Christmas and a dose of small town charm - and the potential for a lot of family drama.

Lee Davis is about to marry the man of her dreams - and at her favourite time of year. But she's finding it hard to feel the magic of Christmas or the excitement about her wedding as a face from her past reappears and worries about her second time down the aisle surface.

James Knight thought he had everything - the woman

he was destined to be with, an adorable daughter and a happy life in the countryside. But with his wife-to-be seeming more and more distant, is he doomed to be jilted at the alter again?

Beth Davis is pretty sure she's lost her heart to handsome, brooding Caspian - but he's moved away to Edinburgh, and their fiery romance seems to have been stopped before it had truly started.

Caspian Blackwell wants to be excited about his promotion and moving to an vibrant new city - but his heart is very much back in Dartmouth.

Can a festive Devon wedding make this the Best Christmas Ever?

Trouble In Tartan

Beth Davis didn't plan on falling in love when she moved to Dartmouth - she just wanted to feel some fireworks. The problem is, she's pretty sure that is exactly what is happening - but the object of her affections is living 600 miles away in Edinburgh. As she tries to start a career as an author, downs a few too many glasses of wine and attempts to make ends meet, keeping a long-distance relationship alive proves more and more challenging.

Caspian Blackwell has never let his heart make big decisions - but he's sorely tempted when the distance between them begins to cause problems in his relationship with Beth. When he decides he wants all or nothing, can he really put this new relationship before his career? Or will he end up exactly where he always feared he would: heartbroken?

A tale of love, longing and a relationship stretched between coastal England and Scotland.

Summer Of Sunshine

A summer holiday can wash up a whole host of family dramas...

Lee Knight wants to relax on a summer holiday away with her husband, sister and brother-in-law. But her desire for another baby is not making it easy to unwind.

James Knight hates to see his wife upset, and hopes a trip away will make her troubles lessen. But with concerns about his father's health, he's finding it hard to be there for her as much as she really needs.

Beth Blackwell is sick to death of everyone asking her two questions: when is her next book coming out, and when is she going to have a baby. The first is proving more difficult than she expected, and the second - well, she's not sure whether that's the way she wants her life to go.

Caspian Blackwell is enjoying life as a newlywed in Edinburgh - although in his heart, he's missing living in Devon. A spate of redundancies at work has him pondering his future - but he worries his new wife's heart is engaged elsewhere when she becomes increasingly distant.

Can sun, sea and sand send the two couples back into

more harmonious waters?

Healing The Heartbreak

Isla Blackwell thought she knew what love was.

But when her five year relationship ends in heartbreak, no home, and no job, she decides to take up her cousin's offer of a break in beautiful coastal Devon.

She expects sea, sand and perhaps some confort for her shattered soul - but when she starts taking shifts at a local bookshop, could love be on the cards?

With the guidance of her cousin Caspian and the rest of his family, as well as the handsome Luca, can Isla heal her broken heart?

'Healing the Heartbreak' is Book Seven in 'The South West Series', but can be read as a standalone novel.

BOOKS BY THIS AUTHOR

The Love Of A Lord

When grieving hearts find each other, can love overcome secrets, vows and society's expectations?

Compelled to uncover the secret surrounding her mother's death, Annelise Edwards unexpectedly finds herself the guest of the handsome Lord Gifford.

Lord Nicholas Gifford has no interest in women after being jilted by his betrothed, but he cannot ignore his sense of duty when a mysterious woman appears on his doorstep during a terrible storm and falls ill.

As they wait for the storm and Annelise's fever to pass, they are forced to share the grief that is weighing on both their hearts. And when Nicholas becomes more involved in Annelise's efforts to piece together her mother's past, it becomes increasingly difficult to deny their blooming attraction.

Will Nicholas give up the lonely life he has become accustomed to? And will it even matter once he finds out Annelise's mother was nothing but their maid?

If you like your rags to riches romance mixed with Tudor drama, you'll love this heart-warming first novel in the touching The Hearts of Tudor England series.

The Love of a Lord is book one in The Hearts of Tudor England series, and can be read as a standalone novel.

Can't Let My Heart Fall

When a marriage is arranged for Alice and Christopher, love was never part of the bargain.

Alice Page long ago swore she would never fall in love. After watching her father's heartbreak at the death of her mother, and Queen Katherine's pain at her husband's philandering, it just doesn't seem worth the pain.

Marriage to Christopher Danley, however, makes keeping that solemn vow to herself somewhat difficult. In the daytime she can keep her distance, but at night she realises she has never felt closer to another human before.

Lord Christopher 'Kit' Danley knows he will be an Earl one day, but he plans to spend every moment of the time before that happens travelling the seas and discovering new lands. When his father delivers an ultimatum, marriage is the only option – but never did he imagine he would find marriage as enjoyable as he does with Lady Alice.

With Alice panicking at realising her heart may be lost

to the handsome Kit Danley, and Kit called away on the King's business, can love flourish in this marriage of convenience?

Can't Let My Heart Fall is book two in The Hearts of Tudor England series, and can be read as a standalone novel.

Misrule My Heart

When Isabel realises over the Twelve Days of Christmas that she cannot marry the man she is required to, will she follow her family's wishes or her heart's desires?

Isabel Radcliffe knows she must marry well. As the daughter of a merchant who has risen at court, many opportunities are within her grasp - and marrying a Lord is one of them.

When her father hosts nobility over the Twelve Days of Christmas, she knows she will meet the man he wishes her to marry, and begin the life that has been laid out before her.

What she does not expect is for him to be quite so old or quite so unpleasant...

Suddenly, the duty binding her to such a life-changing decision feels like too much of a sacrifice. And when her head and heart are turned by the dashing and daring stable lad Avery, she questions whether she can follow through with her father's wishes.

A tale of love, duty and the magic of Christmas, with a

dose of Tudor drama.

Misrule My Heart is book three in 'The Hearts of Tudor England' series, and can be read as a standalone novel.

Saving Grace's Heart

Since witnessing her sister's romantic elopement, Grace Radcliffe has been determined to choose her own husband.

And while finding excuses not to marry every man her father has put in her path has worked so far, she knows time is not on her side - and so she sets her sights on the handsome Duke of Lincoln, planning to ensure they are a good match before letting her father seal the deal.

When Harry, the dashing new Duke of Leicester, is put in her path instead, she knows there must be something wrong with him - for her father has never picked well in the past.

But when he helps her in her hour of greatest need, she begins to question that judgement.

Can Grace find the route to true love? Or will her free-spirited ways lead her into a loveless marriage?

Saving Grace's Heart is Book Four in 'The Hearts of Tudor England' Series, and can be read as a standalone novel.

Learning To Love Once More

A widowed Earl, a lonely governess, and a whole lot of heartbreak.

James, Earl of Tetbury, has never known an all-consuming love - but after losing his wife to the perils of childbirth, he resolved not to suffer that pain again.

Fed up of being a burden on her Aunt and Uncle, orphaned Catherine Thompkins decides being a governess will fill the loneliness in her soul and provide her with a modicum of independence. What she is not expecting is to fall in love with the Earl she is working for.

When James realises he and the children need Catherine in order to flourish, he offers marriage - but in name only. There will be no more children, he is resolute about that.

As Catherine falls deeper and deeper in love with the damaged Earl, can she persuade him that love is worth risking your heart for?

Learning to Love Once More is Book Five in 'The Hearts of Tudor England' series, and can be read as a standalone novel.

An Innocent Heart

On the same day as Henry VIII's second daughter is born, Elizabeth Beaufort makes her way into the world. Inspired by the way the Princess lives her life, she vows to live as a maid - no love, no marriage, no children.

But as the Tudor dynasty sends lives in England reeling,

can Bessie Beaufort's heart remain caged?

Edward Ferrers has always known he will marry and carry on his father's merchant business. In fact, such a marriage has been lined up for him for several years - until a chance meeting at the Tudor Court sends his heart racing for Bessie Beaufort.

In a time of courtly love, female purity and religious upset, can Edward persuade Bessie that their love is worth fighting for?

An Innocent Heart is Book Six in 'The Hearts of Tudor England' series, and can be read as a standalone novel.

Let Love Grow

Lady Lily Merriweather has waited a long time for love to blossom. Through the death of her father, the loss of their fortune and their relocation to Bath, she has held steadfast in the opinion that true love will be found. Can she find it right beneath her nose?

Hugh Baxter was rather irritated when his father asked him to keep an eye on his deceased best friend's daughters. But Lady Lily soon becomes a close friend and ally, especially during the Bath season - a dangerous time for any unwed man.

In the elegance and glamour of the season, will Lily and Hugh realise that their feelings for one another are more than platonic?

Printed in Great Britain
by Amazon

20702999R00149